The Ratchet & Bougie Wives of Vegas

A novel by Lady Lissa

Connect with me!

Facebook: https://www.facebook.com/AuthoressLadyLissa

Twitter: https://twitter.com/LadyLissa832

Instagram: lady_lissa832

TikTok: TheRealLady_Lissa

Email: ladylissa832@gmail.com

Prologue

Dior Foster

As I sat in the hospital room next to my mom's bed, I could feel myself ready to break down. My mom had been battling breast cancer for the past seven months, and the type that she had was really aggressive. Triple negative breast cancer was one of the toughest cancers to beat and after four months of treatment, my mom decided that she didn't want to do it anymore. Me and my sisters were devastated when she made that decision because we knew what was coming.

Chemotherapy was hard on her body. She would be sick for days at a time, not only had she lost weight, but she had also lost all her hair. I think that was the worse part of it all. Watching her diminish from the woman who raised me and my sisters to the shell of a woman she was now.

I really thought my mom was going to beat the cancer, especially since the doctors had given a good prognosis with the chemotherapy. That wasn't the case though.

Over the past month, my mom's health had begun to deteriorate rather quickly. I dropped by to check on my mom one day and found her passed out on the kitchen floor. She was barely breathing so I called 9-1-1.

She was rushed to the hospital and had been here ever since. Over the past couple of weeks, things went from bad to worse. My mom wasn't functioning like she was before. She couldn't get out of bed anymore, so a catheter had to be put in. She was on oxygen but still able to speak to me and my sisters.

At that point, me and my sister's made the decision to bring in Hospice. I hated seeing my mom like this. She had always been so strong. She raised me and my sisters by herself and even though we grew up in the projects in fifth ward Houston, she still made sure we had everything we needed. Of course, there were things that we desired and wanted, but she couldn't afford those things, so we did without.

I wasn't mad at her though because I knew that she was doing the best that she could. Unbeknownst to us, our mom had signed paperwork to not resuscitate her if she stopped breathing. We found that out once the huge red 'DNR' sign was put on the whiteboard in her room.

I couldn't believe my mom had made such a decision without talking to us first, but I understood why. She was just tired suffering and she admitted that to us the day before she died.

"Mama if you start the chemo again, you can fight this," Milani said.

She shook her head no. "Too late," she responded weakly.

"It's not too late mom!" Milani cried as she held our mom's hand.

"Tired," mom responded in a voice barely above a whisper. "So tired."

"Let her get some rest Milani," I said as Imani, my other sister stood quietly near the window.

My mom looked over at her and called her name. Imani walked over to the side of the bed and grabbed a tissue from the box. She wiped her eyes as mom stared from one of us to the other. She looked like a skeleton with very little skin on her bones. I didn't know how Milani expected her to fight off such a determined disease. Mom didn't stand a chance.

"I love... y'all so much. Wish I was a better mom..."

"Don't say that mom!" I cried. "You were the best mom to us that you could be, and we love you for that!"

"Yea mommy! We love you so much!" Imani cried.

"I love you mama," Milani said.

"Mama tired," she whispered.

"Then get some rest mom. We will be here when you wake up," I encouraged.

"No," she said as she looked at us with tears in her eyes. "Tired fight-ing. Can't fight..."

It hit me like a ton of bricks when I realized what she meant. She didn't want to fight to live anymore. She was tired fighting to breathe. My heart literally broke into a ton of pieces. Tears erupted from my eyes as I sat and held her hand.

"It's okay mom. You did what you came here to do. You raised us to be strong, independent and smart. We know what we have to do," I cried.

"Love y'all. Dior take care of your sisters," she asked as she looked into my eyes.

"I will mom. I will always look out for them."

After she said that, she closed her eyes and went to sleep. I wasn't sure when she slipped away or what time it was when we fell asleep. All I knew was the machine started blaring letting us know that she had flatlined. I wanted to scream for someone to do CPR and resuscitate her, but that wasn't what she wanted, so they couldn't.

"Mama! Mama don't go!" Imani cried as she erupted in tears. "MAMA PLEASE!!"

"She's already gone Mani!" Milani stated as if she wasn't affected.

A nurse rushed in and turned off the loud machine. Tears spilled from my eyes as I wept for my mom. I couldn't believe our mama was gone. What were we going to do without her?

Chapter one

Dior Foster

After our mom's funeral, me and my boyfriend made the decision to get married and move my sisters to Vegas, which was where he lived. Of course, I was shocked that he had even suggested marriage since we had only been dating a couple of months, but what was the alternative? If I didn't agree to marry Jaylen, me, Milani and Imani would be stuck here in fifth ward in this crappy ass apartment surrounded by all those memories of our mom and our childhood.

So, I agreed. I wasn't in love with Jaylen, but I figured love would come eventually. That was why three days after we buried our mom, the three of us with Jaylen's help, packed up the stuff we wanted to keep and trashed the rest before turning the keys over to the office manager.

Thank God for Jaylen because I didn't know what I would have done without him. Mom didn't have any life insurance, so he was kind enough to pay for the funeral, and it was beautiful. Our mom was buried in a beautiful, white casket with a blush pink interior because that was her favorite color. There were a ton of flowers everywhere and it made me smile because that let me know that our mom was loved by everyone and not just us. We had declined to have a repast dinner because to be honest, I was ready to get out of the hood.

Jaylen and I had met through a mutual friend, and we hit it off right away. He was a little older than me, but he was a great looking man. I would be lying if I said Jaylen's bank account and his need to take care of me weren't also what attracted me to him. As a matter of fact, that was the main reason why I agreed to marry him.

I had been to Jaylen's place before in Las Vegas and I loved being there. The bright lights of the city made me not want to return to Houston. I needed this man, and he wanted me, so it was a win- win for both of us.

I didn't have a father growing up, so when he said he wanted to marry me and take care of me, I jumped at the chance. The past few weeks had been hard on me and my sisters, but the past few days had been harder than anything I had ever experienced in my life. With that being said, we were looking forward to getting the hell out of H-Town.

There were too many painful memories here. It was time for something new and different. On the plane ride to Vegas, me and Milani chopped it up excitedly while Jaylen conducted business on his phone. I noticed how quiet Imani was as she looked out the window. I had flown to Vegas once since me and Jaylen started dating, so I was excited to get back out there. I couldn't wait to get to Jaylen's penthouse in the high- rise complex.

It was like being in a totally different country than where I grew up and lived. Once we got to Vegas, there were two drivers waiting for us at the airport.

"You have two vehicles?" I asked.

"Yes, because there won't be enough room for everyone and all y'all things in one truck," he explained.

As the drivers packed our things in the second truck, we piled into the first one. "So, the two of you are getting married, right?" Milani asked.

"That's the plan," Jaylen said.

"So, are we all gonna be like some sister wives type shit?" Milani inquired with a perplexed expression on her face.

"The hell!" Imani shrieked.

How dare she say something like that! Me and Jaylen weren't even married yet, and she was talking about him paying for them an apartment. I didn't know what the hell had gotten into my little sister, but I was going to find out.

"Not at all!" I interjected. "I'm gonna be Jaylen's wife... period! I promised mom that I'd look out for the two of you and that's why we're all moving to Vegas."

"You could have taken care of us in Houston," Milani responded smartly.

"So, you wanted to stay in the apartment?" I asked as I snaked my neck.

"Oh, hell naw! But Jaylen could have paid for us a better apartment or something!" she stated in a matter- of- fact manner.

"Uh, excuse you!" I shrieked. "

"I'm just saying," she said with a shrug.

Thankfully, the conversation ended as the drivers pulled up in front of the high- rise. The driver opened the door, and we stepped out of the vehicle. As Milani and Imani stared up at the tall building, both their mouths flew open.

"Damn! This where you live?" Milani asked Jaylen.

"Yes," he said as he smiled proudly.

"This is amazing!" Imani said with a smile.

This was the first time I saw her smile since mom passed away. "What floor are we going to be on?" Milani asked.

"The penthouse," Jaylen responded.

Once all the luggage had been piled onto the wheeled cart, Jaylen tipped the drivers, and we headed inside the high- rise. He stopped by the front desk before we made our way to the elevators.

"Good afternoon Mr. McClain. Welcome back!" the desk clerk greeted.

"Good afternoon, Bradley. This is my future wife, Dior and her sisters, Milani and Imani. They will be moving in, so I need you to put them in the books, so there won't be any problems letting them up when they go out," Jaylen explained.

"Yes, sir. If I can just get their identification cards, I can do that right now," Bradley stated.

The three of us reached in our purses and pulled out our ID cards and handed them to him. He made copies of them before handing them back to us.

"Will you be needing extra keys to the penthouse as well, sir?" Bradley inquired.

"Yes, three copies please."

"I will post the extra costs on your account."

"That's fine."

"I can have the keys prepared within the hour. I can either have them delivered to your suite or someone can come down and get them," Bradley explained.

"I'll come get them," Milani quickly offered with a flirtatious smile.

"Okay," Bradley said as he looked at her and returned the smile.

I couldn't help but notice how quickly Milani had captured Bradley's attention. I hoped she didn't come to Vegas to become a thot. I had plans for both of them to go back to school and finish college, but thotting wasn't on my agenda for my younger sisters.

As the young guy pushed the cart towards the elevator, I saw him and Milani sharing admiring glances with each other. I rolled my eyes as the elevator came to a halt. We all filed in, and the guy pressed the 'PH' button to take us to the penthouse. Once we arrived, the doors opened, and we exited.

The guy removed the bags from the cart and set them by the door. After Jaylen tipped him, Milani walked him to the elevator and chatted with him for a few minutes before he returned to where we stood.

"Milani, you and Imani will have to share a room until I can figure something out..."

"What?!" Milani asked with a shocked expression on her face. "So, you live in the penthouse suite but only have two bedrooms!"

"Well, when I moved in, I was a single man, so two bedrooms were more than enough space for me. Trust me, the bedroom that the two of you will be sharing is big enough for y'all and will be extremely comfortable. Now that I'm taking a wife and moving her sisters in with us, I'll start to look for a bigger place," Jaylen said.

"And how long will that take?" Milani asked as she propped her hand on her hip.

"However long it takes!" I snapped. I was becoming annoyed by her attitude. I don't know why you're even acting this way. I mean, the three of us shared a room in the projects our whole lives, so you should be just as grateful as I am right now because this is definitely an upgrade."

"I am grateful..."

"Then act like it!" I stressed to my younger sister.

"I just wasn't expecting us to share a room," Milani complained.

"But you haven't even seen the room!" I argued.

Why was Milani tripping like this? Maybe it was because of all we had been through over the past few days. Maybe she was just acting out because it was her way of dealing with the grief of losing our mom. I didn't know what it was, but she was going to have to do better. I could only be patient for so long.

"Then show me," she said as she crossed her arms over her chest.

Jaylen wheeled their two large suitcases towards the bedroom they would be sharing, and we all followed behind him. As he opened the door and turned on the lights, I smiled at how big and beautiful this room was. It had a huge king- sized bed in it with a chest and dresser. There were also two nightstands on each side with lamps on them. It was really nice.

"There's also an adjoining bathroom over here," Jaylen said as moved over to the bathroom door and opened it.

He turned on the light to reveal a beautiful bathroom. It had a pretty white spa- like tub and a large walk- in shower. "And a walk- in closet."

Jaylen opened the door that led to the closet and turned on the light. He backed away and Milani and Imani went inside to inspect it. Then they came back into the bathroom and smiled.

"I guess this will do for now," Milani said.

"Thank you for inviting us here, Jaylen. I appreciate it," Imani said softly.

"You're welcome. I'll be looking for a bigger place within the next few weeks. This living situation is just temporary," Jaylen assured. "How about you ladies unpack your bags and settle in and then we can go out to dinner?"

"Dinner in Las Vegas! Yaaaaassss!" Milani cheered as she clapped her hands.

"I'm good with that," Imani agreed.

"Cool," I said.

Me and Jaylen walked out of the room and went to his bedroom. I had slept with Jaylen a few times, so I wasn't nervous about being in this particular space with him. After all, we were getting married, so I might as well get comfortable.

"How do you feel?" Jaylen asked as he wrapped his arms around me.

"Grateful to have you," I answered honestly. "I really don't know what me and my sisters would have done without you. I mean, my mom didn't even have life insurance and you stepped in to help us. You basically did everything because we knew nothing about planning a funeral, even though we knew that time was coming. Thank you."

"You don't have to keep thanking me, babe. I wanted to help y'all."

"Are you really okay with my sisters living here?" I asked.

"Yes, why wouldn't I be?" he asked. "I mean, we are all going to be family soon enough."

"Speaking of which, are you sure we're ready for marriage?" I asked.

He looked into my eyes and asked, "Don't you want to get married?"

"I thought about one day getting married. I just never imagined it would be so soon."

"Are you having second thoughts?" he asked.

Of course, I was having second thoughts, but I couldn't tell him that. This man had opened his heart and home to me and my sisters. I had to marry him because he could provide for us. The lavish lifestyle that Dr. Jaylen McClain led was something that I wanted to be a part of. We needed to be a part of it.

"No, no!" I said, quickly dismissing his thoughts. "I want to marry you, Jaylen."

"Okay. I was just making sure. I don't want you to feel as if I'm rushing you."

"How soon are you wanting to tie the knot?"

"Well, we are in Vegas," he said with a wink. "I mean, we can go today, next week, next month. I'm ready now, so it's up to you."

Whew chile! No, this man did not just say today!

"Well, I don't think today is gonna be the day," I said with a laugh.

"I know. I was just saying that I'm ready today," he reiterated. "But whenever you're ready, I'm ready. I just want you to know that."

"Thanks for telling me that. I wouldn't mind going to the chapel to get married, but I don't wanna just run up there in jeans and a shirt to say I do. I want to go shopping for a dress and a veil cuz this is my first and hopefully, only wedding."

"Yea, I'm hoping this is your only wedding too, so I want us to do it right."

"Cool. So, I'll go shopping for a dress and veil this week. I guess we can walk down the aisle in a couple of weeks. Is that okay?" I asked.

"That's fine babe. I'm excited to be your husband," he said.

"I'm excited too."

Nervous was more like it, but I had to tell him what he needed to hear.

"Well, let me give you something to shop with," he said as he reached in his pocket and pulled out his wallet. He pulled out a card and handed it to me. "You can use this card to buy whatever you need."

"For the wedding?" I asked.

"For whatever you and your sisters need or want. That card has no limit..."

"Don't tell me that!" I shrieked happily as I giggled.

"I'm telling you for a reason. I'll give you the number to the car service that I use..."

"You don't have a car?" I asked.

"Yes, it's in the parking garage, but I use my car for work, and I figured since you all don't know your way around, the car service might be a good idea. At least until you learn the different streets and where the shopping centers are and stuff," he explained.

"Okay. Thanks bae," I said as I kissed him.

"You're welcome. Now, how bout we get dressed for dinner."

"I'm with that. I'm hungry."

"Yea, me too," he agreed.

So, that was what we did. We got dressed to go to dinner with my sisters.

Chapter two

Milani Foster

Losing my mom was the worse thing I had ever gone through... well, aside from the loss of my grandparents a few years ago. Our mom raised me and my sisters by herself, so when she passed away, it affected all of us in different ways. I had no idea what we were going to do now that our mom was gone. Then Dior told us that Jaylen wanted to marry her and move the three of us to Las Vegas.

I thought that was crazy because she hadn't known that man a good two months. How the hell could she agree to be his wife when she didn't even know him like that? I wasn't going to worry about that though because that was between her and that man. I was curious about what would happen between her and Knox though.

He was her broke boo that she had been dating for the past six months. I mean, she was dating Knox before she got involved with Jaylen. And if I wasn't mistaken, I heard her on the phone with him before Jaylen called our hotel room to ask if we were ready to leave for the airport.

But that wasn't my business. Dior was my sister, and I would never betray her trust. It didn't matter if I caught her fucking Knox in the bed that she was going to be sharing with Jaylen, he would never hear that shit from me.

Now that our mom was gone, Dior and Imani were all I had left. Yes, Jaylen was awesome to have brought us all the way out here. It would seem as if he was living large out here and we had been missing out. That fact still didn't change my way of thinking though... blood came before everything.

From what I saw just in this high- rise, Vegas had some fine ass niggas in the area! Between Bradley at the front desk and Niko who handled the bags, I would say that I was about to have a damn good time in Vegas.

I went to Jaylen's bedroom door and knocked on it. Dior came to the door in a beautiful shiny mini dress.

"Well, I wanted to ask you where we were going and how to dress, but it must be somewhere fancy for you to be dressed like that!"

"You like it?" she asked as she did a full turn.

"I love it, but I don't think that any of the clothes I brought can compare to this," I admitted.

"Jaylen got me this. He actually purchased several outfits for me. How about I gather a few outfits I think you and Imani might like and bring them to y'all's room?" Dior offered.

"That's fine because we definitely don't have anything this nice and fancy!"

"Okay, give me a few minutes and I'll be right there," she said.

"Okay." I turned and headed back to the room I was sharing with my sister, Imani.

"Where'd you go?" Imani asked. "I thought we were supposed to be getting ready to go to dinner."

"We are, but I went to ask Dior how we need to dress... casual, dressy or bougie."

"What'd she say?"

"Girl, she came to the door with a blinged out dress that would make our lil dresses from Walmart look like a piece of toilet paper!" I stated.

"Wow!"

KNOCK! KNOCK!

"Come in sis!" I called out.

Dior walked in with an armful of stylish and bougie clothes. "Nice dress!" Imani complimented our sister.

"Thanks sis," Dior said as she smiled and placed the clothes on our bed. "So, Milani mentioned that y'all might not have the clothes to go to one of the fancier restaurants, so I brought y'all some of the clothes that Jaylen bought me. If you find something you like and it fits, feel free to wear it."

"What if it doesn't fit?" Imani asked.

"We're about the same size," Dior said as she looked at the two of us.

"We'll see," Imani said as the two of us began to go through the clothes. "Ooooouuuu! I love this!"

Imani chose a short romper and rushed to the mirror to put it up against her. "Just try it on, Imani!" I stated as I rolled my eyes.

"I just wanted to see how it would look in front of me first," she said.

"So, you gonna put the hanger around your neck and wear the outfit like that?" I asked.

Dior busted out laughing but Imani did not find it funny at all. She shut the bathroom door, probably to try the outfit on.

"Girl, you crazy!" Dior said with a laugh.

"I was just asking her," I said as I shook my head. Then I started looking through the clothes and found a dress that I liked.

It was red, fitted and short. I began to remove my clothes and pulled the dress over my head.

"Uhm, you do know it has a zipper," Dior asked as she cracked up laughing.

She unzipped the dress because it wouldn't go over my damn head. Once she unzipped it, I was able to get the dress to slide down my body.

"Zip me! Zip me!" I commanded my sister so she could zip the dress.

After she did that, I knocked on the bathroom door so Imani could let me in. I needed to look at myself in the mirror too.

She opened the door and I cheered for her.

"This outfit looks good on you, little sister!"

"Thanks. I like it," Imani said as I went into the bathroom.

I stood in the mirror and admired my body in this dress. "Damn! I am fyyyyyne!"

I walked back in the bedroom to show my sisters the dress. "How do I look?" I asked.

"You look HOT!!" my sisters commented at the same time.

"Thank y'all!" I smiled widely. "Now, to find a pair of shoes that goes with this."

"What size do you wear?" Dior asked.

"An eight."

"Aw man! I wear a nine," she responded. "It's okay. Wear what y'all have for tonight, and tomorrow we'll go shopping!" Dior produced a credit card and that made me all warm inside.

"Well, alright sis!" I cheered happily.

"We have those sandals from Walmart that I put the rhinestones on," Imani suggested.

"Yea, they are cute," Dior agreed.

"But will mine go with this dress?" I inquired.

"You can always choose something else..." Dior suggested.

"Oh, no ma'am! This is what I wanna wear!"

"Well, I'm gonna let y'all finish getting ready because we will be leaving in about half an hour. Jaylen made reservations at some fancy restaurant," Dior explained.

"Okay, give us fifteen minutes," I promised.

Dior gathered the clothes off the bed and left the room. "Are you sure you don't mind wearing the rhinestone sandals?" Imani asked with an awkward expression on her pretty face.

"Sis, it's not that serious," I assured her. "Those sandals are real cute since you added those rhinestones. Besides, what's the alternative?"

"You're right."

Imani was the quietest one of the three of us. I hoped that she would embrace life and break out of her shell now that we were in a different area. I was definitely looking forward to making my mark in Vegas. I remembered the keys that were supposed to be picked up from the front desk and hurriedly slipped my feet in the sandals.

"See... it looks great with this dress," I told Imani as I went to the mirror to brush my hair into a ponytail and put a little lip gloss on.

When I made a beeline for the door, Imani asked, "Where are you going?"

"To get the keys from downstairs," I replied with a smile.

"Please just get the keys and come back up here," she said with an uneasy expression.

"What's that supposed to mean?"

"I saw you looking at those guys..."

"And! That's why God gave me these brown eyes... to look at men!" I informed her as I batted my eyes dramatically. Imani just shook her head and smirked. "I won't be long."

I rushed out of the room before she could say another word. I headed to the elevator and pressed the button to the first floor. Once the doors opened, I stepped out and went to the front desk. Bradley's facial expression immediately perked up.

"Wow! You look gorgeous!" he gushed with a huge smile of approval.

"Thank you," I said as I returned his smile. "Are the keys ready?"

"Huh?"

"The extra keys Jaylen requested," I reiterated. He still stood there with a blank expression on his handsome face. "To the penthouse."

"Oh! Yes, I have them right here!"

He turned to a drawer and used a key to unlock it. He pulled the small yellow envelope out and handed it to me.

"Thank you," I said as I took it.

"You're welcome."

I turned and walked away, making sure to twist my hips extra hard because I knew he was looking at my ass. I made it to the elevator and when the doors opened, I was shocked to see Zayne, the guy who brought our bags to the room earlier. Instead of stepping off the elevator, he pulled me in.

He wasted no time sticking his tongue in my mouth and I had no problem accepting it. Zayne was hot! He was about 6'1, had a faded haircut with very little facial hair, pretty brown eyes, and nice white teeth. This man had a well- toned body, so I knew he worked out. As his hands rested on my lower back, we kissed like horny teenagers.

Several minutes passed before I realized the elevator wasn't moving. I pulled back from him and asked, "Is the elevator broken?"

"No, I just stopped it for a minute. I'm about to lose my job for you," he admitted.

"Don't do that!" I spoke firmly but with a giggle. "I just got here."

He pressed the 'PH' button on the panel and the elevator started. "So, I gave you my number. When you gon call me?"

"I will call you. What time do you get off?"

"At ten tonight. Where you going looking all beautiful and shit?" Zayne asked.

"My sister's husband is taking us to dinner at some fancy restaurant."

"Aight. Well, hit me up when you get back."

"I will," I promised as the elevator came to a stop.

"Maybe we can go take a walk on the boulevard when you get back," Zayne suggested.

"Maybe," I flirted. "Talk to you later."

"Aight."

I stepped off the elevator to find my sisters and Jaylen waiting for me in the living room. "Where'd you go?" Dior asked.

"Uh, to get the keys!" I stated as I showed her the envelope.

I handed it to Jaylen since they were keys to his place, so it was up to him to distribute them. And he did. He handed one to me, then Imani and then Dior.

"Please do not lose these," he warned.

"We won't," we all responded.

"Y'all ready to go?"

We all responded yes and we headed back to the elevator. As we entered, Jaylen hit the button for the first floor. As we exited and walked towards the exit, Bradley winked at me. I smiled at him and then I saw Zayne. My heart definitely skipped a triple beat for him.

"Your car is right outside, Mr. McClain," Zayne said.

"Thank you."

We continued walking and the sliding glass doors opened automatically once we were in close proximity. As we stepped outside, the driver to the black Chevy Suburban opened the rear door. We all climbed in and he got behind the wheel.

I guess Jaylen had called ahead and let him know where we were going because even though no words were spoken, he knew exactly where to go. He pulled up in front of this fancy place called Oscar's Steakhouse and jumped out to open the door. After Jaylen tipped him, we went inside.

I had never been in a restaurant as nice as this before. After looking at the menu, I wondered if we shouldn't have just gone to Checkers or Burger King. I didn't know shit about no damn lobster, and what the fuck was a filet mignon? I was about to ask a question but then I read that it was beef steak.

I ordered a butter poached lobster tail with mashed potatoes and macaroni and cheese. As I looked around this bougie ass restaurant, I noticed what everyone else was wearing. The sooner we went shopping, the better off we'd be. I couldn't wait because I needed shoes and clothes.

"So, Dior told us that we were going shopping tomorrow. Where do you suggest we shop?" I asked Jaylen.

"What kind of clothes are you ladies looking for?" he asked.

"Shit, I'on know about my sisters, but I want some Gucci, Louis V., Prada, that kinda stuff. I wanna fit in and be bougie and classy too," I said.

"If that's what you all want, then I suggest The Shops at Crystals. That's one of the places I shop often," Jaylen said.

"So, what's our limit? Only asking cuz that shit is pricy!" I informed him.

"No limit! I want the three of you to shop for whatever it is you want whether it's clothes, shoes, jewelry..."

"JEWELRY!!" I shrieked.

"Yes, jewelry!" Jaylen assured as he chuckled. "Another thing you ladies need to do is get new ID cards or driver's licenses with your new Vegas address."

"Don't we need proof of address?" Dior asked.

"Yes, so I'll have my secretary type up a residency form for each of you. You just take it down to the DMV and get them swapped out."

"You thought of everything huh?" Imani finally spoke.

"I'm trying to make sure I don't forget anything. I know that the past few weeks have been rough on you all..."

"Try the past few months," I expressed as I blew out an exasperated breath.

"Yea, I'm just trying to help make your lives a little easier."

"And we appreciate that, Jaylen," Dior said with a smile. "I honestly don't know what we would have done if you hadn't come to our rescue. Even though you haven't known me that long, you still stepped in to help us. You just made everything so much easier."

"I care a lot about you Dior. I hated that the three of you had to go through that, so anything I can do to help, I'm here," he said.

Shit, I was glad he wanted to make things better for us. I was going to take full advantage of that shit too. After growing up in the hood for the past twenty- three years and being deprived of all life had to offer, I was going to accept everything that Jaylen had to offer.

The food was delivered and a drink that I hadn't ordered was placed in front of me. I looked up at the server and said, "I think you delivered this to the wrong table. I didn't order this."

"It's from the gentleman over there," she said as she pointed to a table with about five guys.

They looked like professional ball players here celebrating something. "Who are those guys?" I asked.

"They play for the Raiders," the server said.

"The Raiders?" I inquired with a quizzical expression as I shrugged my shoulders.

"You ever heard of the Oakland Raiders? They're a team with the NFL. A couple of years ago, they moved the team here. Anyway, the guy who sent over the drink to you... his name is Javarius Johnson, and apparently, he's interested in you."

"Oh, well, tell him thanks," I said as I raised my glass in his direction.

"Will do. Enjoy your meals," she said before she left the table.

"Well, look at you," Dior said. "You ain't been here twenty- four hours and you already caught the attention of an NFL player!"

"It's the dress," Imani said as she bumped my arm with her elbow.

"Girl!" I expressed excitedly.

As we all ate our food, I couldn't help but look up at Javarius every so often. He was handsome as hell. He was huge and athletic with muscles I had only seen on the Hulk. His light brown eyes sparkled all the way over here, and when he winked at me, all my insides quivered. That man was fine!

I hadn't been here a full day yet, and I had flirted with Bradley, kissed Zayne and now, a player from an NFL team had treated me to a drink. If this was how my first day was going, I could wait to see how the rest of my week was going to go.

Chapter three

Imani Foster

Never in my life did I imagine myself leaving Houston to live in Las Vegas. The only reason I agreed was because now that my mom was gone and my sisters were willing to move, there was nothing for me in H-Town. Once we arrived in Vegas, I was immediately excited by all the livelihood and people hustling and bustling. The streets were extremely busy, and it seemed as if everyone had somewhere to be.

I wasn't as outgoing as my sisters though. Dior had found herself a rich doctor and was getting married, and Milani was just wild as hell. I mean, we had only been here for a few hours, and she already been caught flirting with at least three dudes. I couldn't even lie... I was a bit jealous that she was like that. getting so much attention.

But then again, I would be more surprised if she didn't get attention because she put herself out there like that.

"You alright?" Jaylen asked me.

"I'm fine."

"You're kind of quiet," he said.

"I'm always quiet," I replied.

"We're going to have to find a way to break you out of your shell. You're in Vegas now, so this is a totally different atmosphere than where you're from," he said.

"Yea, I know. Eventually, I will break out of my shell once I get comfortable with everything. No need for you to worry."

"Okay, great! I just want you to enjoy your time in Vegas."

"I am enjoying my time," I admitted.

"Are you enjoying the food, Imani?" Dior asked.

"Yes, it's very good, but I expected that from a place so fancy."

"When we going to the casino?" Milani asked.

"We can go right now if you want to," came a strong, deep masculine voice from behind us.

As me and my sister turned around, we stared up into the face of the tall, handsome, muscular man who sent over the drink to Milani.

"Excuse you!" Milani shrieked, but I could tell that she was flattered.

"Please excuse me for invading on your dinner. I just couldn't help but notice how beautiful you are. Y'all are all beautiful, but you caught my attention as soon as you walked through the door," Javarius admitted, causing my sister Milani to blush profusely.

"Thank you," she said.

"I know you don't know me from any of these other strange men in here, but I'd like to get to know you. I was walking over here to see if we could exchange numbers, but overheard you say something about going to the casino. I'd like to take you if you'd like," he offered.

"No, she wouldn't!" Dior stated abruptly. "My sister doesn't know you like that!"

"I know, but I can promise you that I won't hurt her. I play for a pro ball team, so trust me when I say, I am not looking for any type of scandal that could throw my career off. I'm just trying to get to know a pretty girl..."

"Fine! I'll go with you," Milani said as she put her napkin on the table.

"Milani! You don't know this man!" I noted.

"You are not going anywhere with this stranger!" Dior fussed.

"Excuse you sister, but I think we buried mama last week," Milani stated as she rolled her eyes and pushed her chair out. "Don't wait up."

I couldn't believe Milani had just walked away with that man. "Why did you let her leave?" I asked Dior.

"I can't stop your sister from leaving. She's grown just like you! What did you expect me to do?"

"Stop her!" I fumed.

"I couldn't have stopped Milani from leaving anymore than I could stop you from leaving if you wanted to. You both are grown, young women Imani."

"Your sister will be fine," Jaylen assured.

"How do you know that?" I asked.

"The guy plays for the Las Vegas Raiders! If something happens to your sister or she goes missing, there are plenty of people here who saw her leave with him. Trust me, he doesn't want that kind of negative publicity or like he said, a scandal. I'm sure Milani will be fine," Jaylen said.

I wished I had his confidence, but we were new to this city. We didn't know anyone but each other, so she should have never left. I said a quick prayer that my sister would return home safely. Her and Dior were all I had left.

"Don't worry, Imani. She'll be okay," Jaylen said as he smiled.

I didn't bother responding. I was pissed!

About thirty minutes later, the server walked over with a black billfold, and I was sure it held the check for restaurant total. She handed it to Jaylen, and he placed his card inside and handed it back to her. She quickly walked away and returned a couple of minutes later and handed it back to him.

He signed, took his card and thanked the server. "Thank you so much. I hope you guys enjoyed your evening and that we see you all again soon," she said as she walked away.

Once we left, I became angry all over again because my sister wasn't with us. I still couldn't believe that Milani had just left that way. On the ride back to the penthouse, I sent her a text message.

Me: Are you okay?

It took her several minutes to respond back, but I was happy she did text me back.

Milani: I'm great sis! Don't worry

Me: How can I not worry? You left with a stranger! We just got here!

Milani: I know but he's so cool! Look

She attached a picture of the two of them at the Blackjack table. They were all hugged up like a couple. I shook my head and rolled my eyes.

Me: Don't stay out too late cuz I'm gonna wait up for you

Milani: I love you little sister, but you don't have to wait up for me. I'm fine and I don't know what time I'll be getting back. Just get some sleep and we'll talk tomorrow

Me: Okay. Please be safe

Milani: I will. Don't worry. (heart emoji)

Me: Love you

Milani: Love you more (kissy face emoji)

Me: (kissy face emoji)

Well, I felt a little better now that I knew she was okay. I just prayed that nothing would happen to Milani. I didn't know what I'd do without her. I loved Dior, but Milani was more like my best friend. She was a year and seven months older than me, so we had always been there for each other. When we were younger, we played together, our mom bathed us together, we went to the same schools together. We just did everything together.

People sometimes thought we were twins because we had the same caramel colored complexion, grey eyes, and wavy hair. Me and Milani also had the same father while Dior had a different father. She also looked like us, but a shade darker. So, while me and Milani were caramel toned, Dior was a milk chocolate toned.

We all had the same build... thick in the buns and thighs but slim waist. My breasts weren't as big as my sister's. I wasn't sure what size Dior's breasts were, but Milani was a double D, and I was a C cup. I loved both of my sisters very much, probably more now than I did before because our mom had passed away. I didn't want to ever lose either one of them.

Once we made it back, Dior asked, "You wanna watch a movie?"

"No thanks. I think I'm just gonna turn in," I declined. "It's been a long day and I'm kinda tired."

"Okay." She walked over to me and hugged me. "I know you're worried about Milani, but I'm sure she's fine. Try not to worry too much sis cuz then you'll have me worrying."

"Yea, she sent me a text. She's fine, and I'm trying not to worry," I admitted.

"Okay, good. Have a good night. Love you."

"Love you too, Dior. Thank you for dinner, Jaylen and for letting us stay here," I said.

"You're welcome. Have a good night," he responded.

"Thanks, you too."

I headed to my bedroom, removed my clothes and went to the bathroom. Since I had taken a shower earlier, all I needed to do was get dressed for bed. I was glad that me and Milani had put our things away earlier. I was just tired, so after I got dressed, I climbed in bed and was about to put my phone on the charger when I thought of something.

I decided I was going to check Milani's Instagram page to see if she had posted anything. She had posted a couple of pictures of herself with Javarius and a video. She definitely looked happy, and if I hadn't known they had just met a couple of hours ago, I would have thought they had known each other a lot longer.

I felt relieved to see that my sister was okay. That would definitely help me sleep better. I placed my phone on the charger and snuggled under the covers. Tomorrow was a new day...

Chapter four

Milani Johnson

I had no idea our first night in Vegas would be this way. When I agreed to go to dinner, I just wanted to get out of the house and explore the city. I had heard so much about Vegas casinos, so one day I hoped I'd get to go. When Jaylen invited us to move here with him, it was like a dream come true. I knew now that I was of age and living in Vegas, there was no way that I wouldn't get to go to a casino.

When I posed the question, the last person I expected to answer me was Javarius Johnson. I had never heard of him because I didn't know a darn thing about football, basketball or baseball. I mean, I knew how to play basketball and baseball, but I didn't know anyone who played for any of the professional teams.

I wasn't going to go to the casino with him, but then I thought about it. He was a good- looking millionaire who seemed very respectful. I would much rather spend the evening gambling at the casino with him than walking the strip with a broke bag boy at the penthouse. Sure, Zayne looked good as hell, and his kiss ignited something inside me, but he helped people with their bags for a living.

If Dior could snag herself a rich plastic surgeon, then I should be able to hang with an NFL ball player. Once we got to the casino, Javarius handed me two thousand dollars in cash.

"What's that for?" I asked.

"Money for you to spend... unless you don't want it," he said.

"No, I want it!" I said with a laugh as I grabbed his hand. "I just didn't know why you were giving it to me."

"So you can gamble."

"Wow! Thank you!"

"You're welcome beautiful. Now, let's go have some fun," he said as he grabbed my hand. "Where do you wanna start first?"

"I have no idea. I've never gambled before."

"Really?"

"Really!"

"Well, I usually play the Blackjack table and the slot machines. Sometimes I play Russian Roulette or craps, but it's up to you," he said.

"How about you choose and then I'll decide after you play a little while," I suggested.

"Okay. I'm cool with that. Shit, you might be my lucky charm," he said as he held my hand and led me to the crap table.

"I don't know anything about this dice game," I admitted with a giggle.

"You just have to roll the dice and the goal is to get seven or eleven. That's all it takes to win."

"That's it?"

"That's it. You wanna try?" he asked.

"No thanks. I'll just watch you," I said.

"Okay, cool." He put some money on the table, and they gave him two stacks of black chips.

"Wait! How much are these black chips worth?" I asked out of curiosity.

"A hundred a piece."

I counted the chips and there were about twenty of them. "So, that's two thousand, right?"

"Yea baby."

"Don't you think you should've started with some smaller chips?" I asked, concerned that he would lose too much.

"Nah, I don't do small anything," he said with a wink.

"Okkuuurr!" I responded with a laugh.

"Just chill and watch."

He rolled the dice and lost the first three times, so he asked me to blow some magic on them. "What?" I giggled.

"Blow on them. You know, like you blowing out birthday candles," he encouraged as he held the dice in his hand.

"Here goes nothing," I joked as I puckered my lips and blew.

He grabbed me around the waist with his left hand and pulled me closer before he threw the dice on the table. "We got a winner!" the man controlling the table called.

"You won?" I asked excitedly.

"Fuckin' right I did!"

I was so excited that I blew on the dice again and again and again, and he won every single time. We played at that table for about an hour before we decided to move on to something else. By the time we left, he had turned two thousand dollars into so much that he needed a tray to carry them in.

"That was exciting! What are you gonna play now?" I asked in a slightly slurred tone.

No one told me that we could drink for free at the casino. I wasn't a drinker, so I chose a strawberry daiquiri as my drink of choice. It was off the chain. By the time we walked away from the crap's table, I had drunk two and was on my third.

"You alright?" Javarius asked.

"Are you kidding? I am having the time of my life!" I admitted with a smile and wink.

He had been flirting with me all night. I figured it was only fair that I did the same. After all, he was handsome and rich. We moved to the Blackjack table and he turned to me and asked if I knew how to play.

"Nope. Never been to a casino before, remember?" I reminded him.

"Well, this is a game you can play at home. All you need is a deck of cards, but anyway, the goal of this game is to beat the dealer. If the dealer has a total higher than you, then he wins. However, if your total is higher or you get twenty- one, you win. Wanna try?" Javarius asked.

"Okay."

So, for the next forty- five minutes, we played Blackjack. We won some hands, and we lost some hands, but at the end of our playing time, I think we walked away with more than we left behind.

"Now what?" I asked.

"Well, you can't come to a casino and not play the slot machines," he said with a smile. "Let's go cash these chips in and we can play slots."

"You don't play slots with chips?"

"Nah, you gotta use cash for those machines."

"Okay."

So, we went to the 'cash out' window and did just that. The woman counted out thirty- two thousand dollars and some change. I was amazed that he had won that much off only two thousand. He handed a stack of bills to me, and I looked at him in shock.

"Now, what's this for?" I questioned.

"That's your cut for helping me win."

"Oh, no! This is yours!" I declined.

"You helped me win it, so it's yours."

"Are you sure?"

"You better take this money and put it in your purse before I change my mind," he joked with a hearty laugh.

I was not about to ask him anything else. I grabbed the stack and stuffed it in my purse.

"You know what? I like you," I admitted. "I'm glad I decided to come out with you cuz I'm enjoying myself a lot."

"I'm glad too. I'm having a great time with you," he replied.

When he pressed his lips to mine, it surprised the hell out of me, but I wanted him to kiss me. It wasn't a full- blown tongue kiss or nothing like that, but it was a nice lip lock that had my toes curling. He led me to the slot machines, and we chose to play the Mega Moolah machines.

"Why'd you choose this one?" I asked.

"Cuz this one wins the most money."

"How do you bet on this?"

"You just slide money into the feeder and play until you run out. You can either bet the minimum or max, but betting the max wins more," he encouraged with a wink.

"Can I get a good luck kiss?" I asked.

"Hell yea!"

He leaned over and pecked my lips, pulling away with a huge smile. I could feel myself blushing as well. The server who had been bringing my daiquiris ever since we arrived brought me another one and handed Javarius his third drink. We sat at the machine and played until the police sirens on my machine started blaring.

I swear I thought I had broken their shit!

"What happened?" I asked as I jumped up.

"YOU WON!!" Javarius hollered as he jumped up and scooped me up in the air. He twirled me around and that was all I remembered.

I woke up in a huge bed in a room I didn't recognize and when I turned to my left, Javarius was next to me. My head was spinning, and I felt like I needed to throw up. I jumped out of bed and made a mad dash for the bathroom. I made it just in time and started vomiting.

My body heaved until I had nothing left to give. I flushed the toilet and grabbed the bathrobe hanging on the back of the door. The gold letters on the front of the robe let me know that I was at Cesar's Palace.

"What the hell am I doing here?" I asked myself as I stood in the mirror trying to remember.

"You alright?" Javarius asked as he came up behind me and wrapped his arms around me.

"Yea, just a little confused. How..."

"First off, I didn't take advantage of you last night. We did not have sex," he said. "That's why we're both still fully clothed and you still have your panties on."

"Uhm, I need to brush my teeth," I said as I covered my mouth.

"That's your toothbrush in the package. I picked it up last night on the way up here, and you can use the toothpaste on the counter."

I grabbed the toothbrush and as I was taking it out of the package, I noticed something shining on my left hand. As I raised my hand up, I noticed a ring on it.

"Uh, Javarius, is there something you wanna tell me?" I asked as I held up my left hand.

He looked up and said, "Oh, we got married this morning."

"Huh?"

"We went to one of those lil chapels and got married. Hey wifey," he said with a huge smile.

"Oh my God! This is not funny!"

"I know but I'm dead serious."

He walked out of the bathroom and into the bedroom. He came back with a gold paper, and sure enough, it was a marriage license.

"No, no, no, no! This cannot be happening right now!" I shrieked.

"I don't see what the big deal is. I mean, sure, it was a spur of the moment decision, and we don't know each other well..."

"Javarius, we don't know each other at all! We just met last night!" I cried.

"I know, and to be honest, this is one of the wildest things I have ever done in my entire life."

"I highly doubt that!"

"No, seriously. I thought about getting married one day, especially since I'm thirty- two and all my other friends and most of my teammates are married with kids."

"You're thirty- two?" I asked.

"Yep, and I've never been married, and I don't have a bunch of baby mamas running around, or any females claiming that I'm their baby's daddy! My parents are married and have been for thirty years. I have two sisters and three brothers, and sometimes, I go to church with my whole family," he explained.

"Lemme brush my teeth and get myself together cuz we need to talk about this! My sisters are going to give birth to cows when I tell them this shit!"

"I'll be waiting for you in the bedroom."

He walked out of the bathroom and shut the door. I looked at the plain gold band on my finger and shook my head side to side. This could not be happening for real! This was some crazy ass shit!

I grabbed the toothpaste and put some on the toothbrush. Then I stood before the mirror and cleaned my dirty ass mouth. I kept looking at the ring that had bound me to this man for the rest of my life. How did we end up getting married? How did we end up at some chapel?

After I finished making myself more presentable, I walked back out to the bedroom. Javarius was sitting on the bed looking out the window. From the room we were in, we could see all of Vegas. I could even see the high- rise that I was supposed to live in with my sisters.

"I need to use the bathroom and brush my teeth. I won't be long," he said.

I nodded my head but didn't say anything. As I stood near the window and looked out at the city, it didn't look the same as it did last night. There were no bright lights, no street traffic and my phone was ringing like crazy.

I must have been in a daze before because I just heard it. I rushed over to my purse and pulled it out. I looked at the wad of cash on the dresser and in my purse and shook my head.

"Hello," I answered.

"Milani where the hell are you?" asked Imani in a worried tone.

"Sis, calm down. I'm fine."

"That doesn't answer the question! You didn't come home last night, and I've been worried sick, especially since I've been calling you all morning and you haven't been answering! Where the hell are you?"

"I'm fine and I'll explain everything to you when I get back."

"And when will that be?" she asked angrily.

"Give me a couple of hours," I said.

"A couple of hours! Milani..."

"Imani please! Stop acting like you're my mama!" I yelled.

"I'm sorry," she said softly. I could tell that she was ready to cry, so I quickly apologized to her.

"No, I'm sorry. I didn't mean to yell at you, but you're starting to freak me out!"

"I've just been so worried about you."

"I know, and I'm sorry I made you worry. I promise I'll be home in a couple of hours, and I'll explain everything to you then."

"You promise?" Imani asked in an uncertain tone.

"I swear!"

"Okay. Two hours!"

"Two hours," I affirmed.

We ended the call as Javarius stepped out of the bathroom. "Everything okay?" he asked.

"Yea, my sister was worried about me."

"Sorry about that," he said.

"It's not your fault. Can we talk about this marriage though?"

"Are you hungry? Because I can eat," he stated with a smile.

"I am but I think we need to talk about this first before we go anywhere."

"How about we talk over breakfast? I'll order room service," he suggested.

"Okay."

So, we looked over the menu and he made the call once we decided what we wanted to eat. Twenty minutes later, there was a knock on the door, and he went to get it. One of the hotel workers walked in with a silver tray on wheels. Javarius handed her a tip and she walked out.

He set the plates on the table and took the lids off. I had ordered a bacon, ham and cheese omelet with white toast and fresh fruit and a glass of orange juice. Javarius had a whole spread of bacon, ham, sausage, grits, scrambled eggs, toast and fresh fruit with two glasses of orange juice.

"Are you sure you're gonna eat all that?" I inquired with a raised brow.

"Babe, I'm a grown man!" he assured me. "Now, let's talk about what you wanna do now."

"It's not up to just me, but I don't see how we can make this work. We don't know each other."

"Well, let's get to know each other then."

"This right here is not going to make us being married work," I said.

"Then what will?"

"I don't know. What I do know is that my sisters are going to kill me!"

"Really? You don't think they'll be happy for you?" Javarius asked.

"We just lost our mom last week," I said sadly.

"I'm sorry about that. Was she ill?"

"Yea, she had breast cancer. We literally found out seven and a half months ago, and now she's gone. Like, I'm not even from here. Me and my sisters literally just moved here yesterday!"

"Word!"

"Yea. So, how do you think they're gonna feel when I go home and tell them that I got married to a stranger last night?" I pondered.

"I'm not sure how they're gonna feel. I mean, I'm also gonna have to break this news to my family. Look Milani, I don't know what you wanna do, but maybe you should take the time to get to know me better instead of just writing me off and saying we can't do this," he said as he stared into my eyes.

"What are you saying?"

"I'm saying let's stay married. If you don't wanna move in with me and do all the things married couples do right now, that's cool. We can take it slow and date. I'd like you to move in my place with me, but if you prefer to live with your sisters, I'm open to that as well," he suggested.

"Why?"

"Why what?"

"Why do you wanna stay married to a woman you don't know?" I inquired.

"Because I really like you. I felt a spark when we kissed the first- time last night, and I've been feeling it ever since. You can't tell me that you haven't felt it too cuz I know you have," Javarius stated with a serious expression on his handsome face.

Looking at him right now, in this beautiful morning sunlight, he reminded me of the rapper, David Banner. He was sexy as fuck, and he was also a gentleman. Even though we got married last night, he never crossed the line and had sex with my drunk ass. He had no idea how many points he scored just for that.

"I might have felt a little something," I admitted as I felt my cheeks heat up.

"Look, if you really wanna dead this thing before it goes any further, I can have my attorney draw up papers to get the marriage annulled. However, if you would like to give our marriage a shot, that's what I want too," he admitted.

I could not believe I was even considering this. I did not know this man. "I have one question."

"Shoot!"

"How many hoes you been fucking?"

He started choking on his food and quickly grabbed his glass of juice. Once he calmed down, he looked up at me and asked, "Huh?"

"You heard me. How many bitches you been having sex with? I know it's a personal question, but I need to know what I'm getting myself involved in," I explained.

"Well, as of recently, one... maybe two," he replied as he held up two fingers.

"Maybe two?"

"Okay, two, but it wasn't anything serious," he quickly added.

"Maybe not serious for you, but how do you know it wasn't serious for them?"

"Well, if it was, they're gonna have to get over it cuz I's married now," he said jokingly.

"Ha! HA! I'm not playing about this Javarius! I can't be married to a man who is gonna cheat on me, and that's what you pro ball players do!"

"I don't cheat!"

"You already admitted to fucking two women!" I reminded him.

"But neither of those relationships are relationships. They're just jump offs," he said.

"Well, I won't sit back and let you make a fool of me with jump offs either," I said.

He stood up and walked over to me and sat in the chair next to me. He took my hand in his and linked our fingers together. As he stared into my eyes, I could feel my lady part throbbing.

"If you decide to give this marriage a shot, I will too. It'll be just me and you," he said seriously.

"I still don't know if that's..."

He pulled me closer and pressed his lips against mine, this time, he added his tongue. I couldn't help but open my mouth and kiss him back. Damn! Now, he had my whole insides on fire!

I quickly pulled away from him as a slow smile crept across his handsome face. "That's why we should give this a try cuz I know you feel that shit too," he said.

"Fine! I can admit it, but don't think you gon play me for a fool," I warned as I wagged my finger.

"You better put that shit away before I bite it off," he threatened jokingly. "So, does that mean we go full swing and I show you where you will be living from now on or do you wanna take it slow and still live with your sisters?"

Either way, I'd have to share a bed. The question was who did I want to share it with... my sister or my husband?

My husband. I had a fucking husband!

"Can you show me where we'll be living?"

"Weighing all your options... smart," he clowned. "But yea, I can take you there right now if you wanna go."

"I do cuz I promised my sister that I'd come home and explain why I stayed out all night to her in a couple of hours," I explained.

"That's cool. Oh, one more thing, that ring ain't real, so before we go to tell your sisters the good news, I'm gonna have my jeweler meet us at the house."

"Your jeweler?"

"You didn't' think I shopped at Jared's, did you?" he asked with an amused expression on his face.

"Frankly, I hadn't even thought about it."

"Well, let's get out of here so we can go tell your sisters the good news!" he cheered.

The good news. It may have been good news for us, but I had a feeling my sisters were not going to feel the same way. However, once we got to Javaius' estate... yea, estate because that was exactly what this was. And once I saw where he wanted me to live, it didn't matter what my sisters had to say.

I had arrived...

Chapter five

Javarius Johnson

The last thing I expected last night when I approached Milani's table was that we'd wake up in my hotel suite married. But we had so much fun last night and after she won that twenty- five thousand dollars on the slots, she was feeling real good.

"I wish things could stay like this forever," she commented.

"They can. Let's get married," I suggested in a playful way.

"What?"

"You heard me. Let's go to the little chapel around the corner and get married."

"Boy bye!" she shrieked and laughed. "I am not about to play with you!"

"You scared?"

She stepped into my personal space and said, "I ain't scared of nothing."

"Prove it."

"How? By marrying you?"

"Yep."

"Okay, I'll bite," she said and burst into laughter. I think at the time, she thought I was joking and maybe I was. But I was going to see just how far this shit would go for us.

We walked out of the casino, and I had my driver take us to the chapel around the corner. Once inside, we presented our IDs, and she couldn't stop laughing. I knew she was a little tipsy and that was okay. If she wanted to get the marriage annulled the next day, we could do that. For right now, I thought it was something fun for us to do.

The ceremony was quick, but the kiss that sealed our union was not. That kiss set off a slew of fireworks inside me and I knew that I wasn't about to let this woman go. I knew I wasn't in love, but no woman had ever made me feel this way before. I was willing to do whatever I had to for her to not leave me.

I had no idea how Whitney or Javante was going to take the news, but that was on them. I was never in any real relationship with them anyway. We were just three friends who got together for some fun... sometimes together and sometimes separately. Either way, they were going to have to move around because I was taken.

After we got married, we headed back to the hotel. I could have gone home but didn't want to bring Milani there without her permission. The last thing I needed was a woman hollering that I had kidnapped her or something. I had been dealing with scandals for years and had finally gotten my reputation to a very good place with the bloggers and reporters.

Wait until they hear the news about this marriage. The press was going to have a field day!

After we made the decision to stay married, I took Milani to my home because I hoped this was where she would choose to live. The only women who had ever been to my house before were my mom, sisters and cousins. I had never brought a woman I was only fucking here because this was my sacred spot where I rested my head at night.

I did not need any drama coming to my doorstep because then it would disrupt my peace, and I wasn't looking for that. I had been with the NFL for since I was twenty- two years old... fresh out of college. First, I signed with the New Orleans Saints, then I got signed to the Oakland Raiders. When the decision was made to move the team to Las Vegas, I was cool with that because I had always wanted to live there.

I bought the perfect house with the most breathtaking view of the city, so all I needed was a wife. And now that I had one, I needed kids. But we could hold off on that for a few years since we had just done some *Married at First Sight* kind of thing. I always heard my mom and sisters talk about that show and wondered how two complete strangers could get married without seeing each other until they were at the altar.

At least me and Milani had spent several hours together before we decided to tie the knot. On the drive to my place, I hit up my jeweler and asked him to meet me there with some of his best pieces of jewelry for married people. He was speechless for such a long time, I had to make sure he hadn't hung the phone up.

"Juan are you there?"

"Yes, I'm here. I guess I'm a little shocked that you asked for wedding pieces. That's all."

"Yea, so can you come by as soon as possible please?" I inquired.

"Sure. Just let me get a few things together and I'll be on my way shortly."

"Thanks, bruh. I knew I could count on you."

"Always Javarius. See you soon."

I ended the call and Milani looked over at me. "I still cannot believe this," she said.

"Believe this," I said as I kissed her again.

A couple of minutes later, we separated, and both blew out heavy breaths. "Whew!" she expressed as she fanned herself. "Boy you better stop it!"

"It is taking everything I have in me to behave with you," I admitted as I kissed her neck.

"Didn't I say stop?" She giggled as she smacked me on the arm.

The driver pulled into the circular driveway of my home and Milani looked over at me with her mouth wide open.

"You live here?" she asked.

"Yep."

"No lie!"

"No lie," I said with a chuckle.

The driver stepped out of the vehicle and made his way over to my door to open it. I stepped out and extended my hand to Milani to help her. The driver shut the door and I handed him a fifty-dollar- bill and a handshake.

"No, fa real! This is where you live!" Milani questioned as I linked my fingers with hers.

"C'mon."

I led her to the door and unlocked it. I turned off the alarm system as Evita came rushing over.

"Oh, Mr. Javarius, it's you!" she expressed as she placed her hand over her chest.

"Yes, it's me Evita. Were you expecting someone else?" I asked.

"No, no! There was a woman who came by looking for you," Evita explained.

"A woman? Did she say who she was?"

"No, just that she was looking for you and saw you with another woman. She was very upset!" Evita stated. "She did not want to leave, so I had to threaten to call the police!"

"Oh wow!" Milani expressed. "What type of shit did you put me in, Javarius? I mean, I have no problem kicking a bitch's ass, but I wasn't trying to come out here and do all that. I would have prepared to leave that shit back in the projects in Houston."

"Chill! You won't be fighting anybody!" I stated. "I'll find out who came here and get the shit straightened out.

I had no idea who could have found their way over to my house because I never told anyone where I lived. All I had to do was pull up the cameras and I'd be able to see who it was.

"Evita, this is Milani. Milani, this is Evita, our housekeeper," I introduced.

"Our, Mr. Javarius?" Evita asked with a lifted brow.

"Yes, Evita. Me and Milani got married last night... well, technically, early this morning, but late last night. You know what I mean."

"Oh my! You are married!" Clearly, Evita was shocked, and it showed on her face. "Well, congratulations to you both! Nice to meet you, Mrs. Johnson. Please let me know if I can do anything to make you more comfortable."

"Aw, thank you so much. You can call me Milani please."

"Okay, Mrs. Milani. Can I get something for you both to drink?" Evita asked.

"Some iced tea would be nice," Milani said.

"Coming right up." Evita rushed off to the kitchen as I turned and wrapped my arms around my wife.

"I can't believe you live here. This is gorgeous!" she expressed with a huge smile on her face.

"You haven't seen anything yet. Wait until I give you the grand tour," I said.

"Then show me."

DING DONG! DING DONG!

"I will as soon as Juan leaves," I promised as I pecked her lips.

I held her hand and opened the door for Juan. "Hey there Javarius," he greeted with a brotherly hug.

"What's up Juan? Thanks for coming over so quickly," I said. "I really appreciate you."

"Well, I had to come by to see who the lucky lady is."

"Well, this is Milani, my wife. Milani, this is my good friend and jeweler, Juan."

Milani stuck her hand out and Juan shook it. "Nice to meet you, Juan."

"Nice to meet you as well, Milani. You are very beautiful. I can see why Javarius wifed you up," Juan complimented.

"Thank you." Milani beamed as she held my hand tightly.

"Well, I have some very impressive pieces that I think the two of you will love. Shall we sit?" Juan asked.

"Yes."

I led the way to the formal dining room, and we took a seat in the chairs. Evita entered the room with coasters and tall glasses of iced tea for all three of us.

"Thank you, Evita," I said.

"You are welcome. Let me know if you need anything else," she said as she scurried along.

Juan opened his briefcase and pulled out several large diamond rings in a glass tray. Milani looked at them and turned to me.

"These are huge!"

"I know."

"You don't have to get me anything that big!"

"Are you kidding? You're the wife of Javarius Johnson, so you deserve it!"

"But it looks expensive," she whispered.

"Babe, it is."

"It's too much."

"Juan, can you excuse us for a minute."

"Yea, sure."

I stood up and pulled out Milani's chair. I held her hand and led her to the master bedroom for some privacy. Once I shut the door, I turned to her as she looked around the huge room.

"Babe, what's wrong?" I asked.

"This is all just too much!" she cried as tears slipped from her eyes.

"Whoa! Whoa! Whoa! I thought you were happy and wanted this to work," I said in confusion.

"I do. But it's just such a drastic change! You have no idea the life I've led before I moved here!"

"I know, and we can talk all about ourselves later. Juan is a very busy guy, and he made time to come all the way out here for us. I know it can be overwhelming..."

"It is. I wasn't expecting any of this!" she cried. "This bedroom is the size of our whole apartment back in Houston!"

"I live well babe. Over the years, I've made some really good investments, so I'm living my best life. I'm sorry you had a hard life back home, but you don't have to struggle with anything anymore. Not ever again because you have a husband now. You can lean on me," I encouraged as I pulled her close. "Now, come on. Let's not keep Juan waiting any longer. And remember, pick out whichever one you want. I can afford it. WE can afford it!"

With that, I lifted her chin and kissed her.

"You good?" I asked.

"Yea, I'm great!" she stated with a smile.

I brushed away her tears and led her out of the bedroom and back to the dining room. "Sorry about that bro," I told Juan as we sat back down.

"It's cool. Y'all good?" Juan inquired.

"Yea, we straight. This is just overwhelming for her. She actually just moved to Vegas yesterday, and now she's married."

"I can imagine how overwhelming it might be, but you married a good dude," Juan said as he looked at Milani. "I've been knowing Javarius for years and he's a solid one."

"Thanks for saying that bro."

"Nah, it's the truth. He'd give any man the shirt off his back, ya know. You got a good one, so you will be fine," Juan continued.

"Just nervous. I've never been married before. And I've never, never seen anything like this before," Milani said as she pointed to the rings. "They're all so big and beautiful."

"Nothing but the best for my wife," I said.

"I don't know which one I like the most," Milani admitted. Then she turned to me. "If you would have asked me to marry you, which ring would you have chosen?"

"Babe it's not about me. It's about you. Most women don't get to pick their own..."

"Right. Their man usually picks the ring, gets down on one knee, and pops the question. However, we did things a little backwards. I just wanna know which ring you would have picked if you would have proposed the right way," she said.

"Okay." I looked at the beautiful rings that Juan had brought and tried to make a decision. Then I saw it. It was a huge pear- shaped diamond in a champagne color set in rose gold with a large diamond on each side. "I choose this one."

"Really?" Milani asked with a huge smile.

"Yea. It's big and different. I've never seen a diamond this color before."

"That's starting to be a popular diamond color," Juan admitted. "It's an eight- carat pear cut champagne diamond with baguettes on each side set in fourteen carat rose gold. It's one of my favorite pieces."

"What size?" I asked.

"Six."

"What size do you wear?" I asked Milani.

My graduation ring is a five and a half..."

"Perfect!" I cheered. I got down on one knee and Milani started giggling.

"What are you doing?" she asked.

"You asked which one would I pick if I had to ask you to marry me, so I figured I'd do it the right way. I mean, I know that we just met, and this new chapter is a scary one for you. Hell, it's scary for me too, but I'm also excited about what the future holds for us. I ain't never been nobody's husband before. I didn't even think I wanted to be a husband until last night. I know this is ass backwards, but I wanna try this marriage thing with you Milani. I know that we're already married, so I'd like to ask you if you'll continue this journey with me and see where it goes. So, Milani I'm asking you to be my wife. Will you?"

Tears were spilling from her eyes, and I could feel myself tearing up as well. "Yea," she agreed.

I took the ring out of the box, slipped it on her finger and kissed her. Juan and Evita clapped their hands as they watched the two of us. What was it about this woman that had me feeling like the luckiest man in the world?

Once the two of us stopped sucking each other's faces, Evita and Juan congratulated both of us. Then Juan said, "Now that the two of you are official, I think it's time we put a ring on your finger too, Javarius!"

"Most definitely!" I agreed as I sat down with my wife. Juan handed me another ring which caused me some confusion. "This is too small for me."

The four of us laughed before he said, "It's not for you. You and your wife are married now, so she needs a wedding band to go with that rock. That's the one that was designed for the ring you chose."

"Oh, okay."

So, Milani pulled the big diamond off and I placed a band of champagne- colored diamonds on her finger before she replaced the other ring. She held her hand up to the light and said, "This is amazing!" She grabbed both sides of my face and placed her lips on mine. "Thank you so much!"

"You're welcome wifey," I said with a smile.

Then we turned our attention to the male rings that Juan had placed on the table. "Wait a minute!" I spoke loudly. "I thought we were getting a ring for me!"

"These are men's rings," Juan said with a chuckle.

"Oh, well, I don't need no big flashy diamonds like that. I just need a nice black gold band or something like that with a few diamonds. This shit here looks like Gucci Mane's wedding band! I ain't trying to be that nigga!" I declined.

"Oh, I just thought you wanted to match your bride's swag," Juan joked. "I should have known better."

"You should have," I stated with a smirk.

"In that case, I got the perfect ring for you bro!" Juan reached inside his briefcase and pulled out a box. When he opened it, I smiled because that was the type of shit I wanted. "This is a black gold and black diamond wedding band, and it just so happens to be your size."

Juan removed the ring from the box and handed it to me. I slipped it on my finger and smiled even bigger. "Yeeeeeaaahh!! That's what I'm talking about! It's like this ring was made for me!"

"It does look good on you," Milani said with a smile.

"Yes, it really does!" Juan agreed.

"Okay, I'll take them!"

"Great! Let me write out your receipt and I'll be out of you lovebirds' hair. So, are y'all planning to go on a honeymoon before y'all start training for the new season?" Juan asked as he wrote my order down on the receipt book.

"We haven't really talked about a honeymoon, but if my wife wants to go on one, that's exactly what we're gonna do," I said as I looked at Milani.

She didn't say anything as she smiled widely. Juan handed me the receipt and I pulled out my wallet for my Black card. I handed it to him, and he processed the payment and sent the receipt to my email. Once he packed up the diamond boxes, he stood up to leave.

Me and Milani walked him to the door hand in hand. I shook and hugged Juan and said, "Thank you so much for coming on such short notice, bro."

"You're welcome. Milani, welcome to the family," Juan said as he embraced her. "Hopefully, your husband will be calling me for some beautiful pieces for your neck, ears, and wrists."

"You already know!" I assured Juan.

"We'll talk soon," Juan said.

"Count on it."

We waved goodbye to him, and Javarius shut the door. "I hate to cut the party short, but I promised my sister I'd be there over half an hour ago. She's been calling but I haven't answered. The last thing I want is for her to file a missing person's report."

"C'mon! You really think she would do that?"

"YES! The way she sounded last night, she was ready to file one then!" Milani expressed.

"Well, we definitely don't want that. Just let me change into some fresh clothes and we can head out," I said as I kissed her.

I ran back to the bedroom, and quickly changed into a pair of Nike basketball shorts and a Nike t-shirt. I stuck my feet in my black Air Jordan's and sprayed some Armani Beauty Aqua di Gio cologne and made my way back to the front room.

"Evita!" I called because I didn't know where she was.

"Yes, Mr. Javarius," she called from upstairs.

"Me and Milani are going to go talk to her family about our marital situation..."

"They don't know?" she asked as she finally made her way to the bottom of the stairs.

"No, they don't, so wish us luck."

"Does Ms. Evelyn and your siblings know?"

"No one knows except you and Juan," I admitted.

"Oh, well, I feel special," Evita said as she touched her heart and blushed.

"You are special, Evita."

"Thank you, and good luck," she said with a smile. "I believe that God put the two of you together for a reason. Don't let him down."

"We'll try not to," I said as I draped my arm across Milani's shoulder and kissed her forehead.

"I will probably be gone before you get back, so I will just see you two in the morning."

"Okay. Thanks for all you do," I said.

"You're welcome."

We headed out to the garage and climbed in my silver metallic Mercedes G- Wagon. I always promised myself that if I ever made it to the big leagues, I was going to buy this truck. And that was exactly what I did.

"I did not know you had a six- car garage!" Milani shrieked as she climbed into the truck.

"There's a lot I haven't shown you babe, but when we get back, I'll show you everything!"

"This house is so big! Why do you have such a big house for just yourself?" she asked as I backed out of the garage.

"Because I knew one day, I wanted to bring a wife here and that we'd eventually have children. I bought this house with a purpose," I explained.

"How long you been having it?"

"I just closed on it two years ago. I had a smaller crib before. I think it was like four thousand square feet."

"And how big is this one?"

"Like eight- five hundred..."

"Eight thousand square feet!" She gasped with her mouth open.

"It's a house for me and our family," I said with a smile. I was about to say my family, but I wanted her to know I was in it for the long haul. "What do you think your sisters will say?"

Before she could respond, her phone started ringing again. She picked up and said, "I'm on my way right now." Silence on the other end before she said, "I'll be there in twenty minutes." Then she hung up.

"Your sister?"

"Yes. I can tell you right now, Imani is going to lose her shit!"

"You don't think she'll be happy for you?" I asked.

"Do you think your family will be happy when they find out that you married a stranger?" she countered.

"I think my mom will be excited because she's been asking for a daughter- in- law," I said.

"Right, but I bet she wasn't expecting you to pick one off the restaurant menu," Milani joked as she giggled.

"Stop it!" I laughed. "But seriously, I just want everyone to be happy for us. I mean, we seem to be embracing the idea just fine. I see no reason why anybody else should have a problem with it."

He pulled up to the high- rise and said, "Damn! This is nice!"

"Yea, it's cool."

"I've seen this high- rise before, and wondered what it looked like inside. It's a pretty, new development too. Only been around for about three years," I explained. "I supposed I need to park in the parking garage."

"Yea, but you can just park on the first floor cuz he lives in the penthouse, so I don't know if you can park all the way up there."

"I can park up there as long as you have a key. "Do you?"

"Yea, I got one."

"Then we good," I said as I headed up to the top floor. "This dude living the life!"

"Yea, but his apartment only has two bedrooms, so me and Imani were gonna share a room," she explained.

"Oh word!"

"Right. I came out here thinking I'd have my own room since me and both of my sisters were grew up together in a two bedroom apartment."

"I wanna hear all about your life in Houston," I said.

"Nothing to tell. We were poor, but my mom was the best mom we could have asked for. She took care of us the best way she could until she couldn't," she said with tears in her eyes. "She passed away and now we're here."

"Okay." I could tell she didn't want to speak about it anymore, so I wasn't going to push her. I parked the truck and we exited.

Once we were outside, I wrapped my arms around her and held her close. She held me tight for a couple of minutes and said, "Come on. Let's get this over with."

We held hands as we headed inside the building. She unlocked the door that led to the inside hallway and took a deep breath.

"Here goes nothing…"

I prayed her family would be okay with this marriage because I was really trying to be positive. Even though I was still in shock that this had actually happened, I was going to do my best to be a good husband to Milani. Hopefully, she would let me.

Chapter six

Imani

When I woke up this morning and saw that my sister hadn't made it hope, I immediately became worried. She promised she would be home by the time I woke up, and she wasn't. So, I grabbed my phone and called her. No answer. I hung up and called again. Still no response. I sent a text message and left a voicemail, but she didn't respond to either.

By the time she finally did answer, I was going out of my mind with worry. I hadn't told Dior that Milani hadn't come home because there was no need for both of us to worry, but when she hadn't shown up after two hours, I felt like I didn't have a choice but to tell Dior.

"Why didn't you tell me this sooner?" she asked in a worried tone.

"I don't know! I just assumed she would come home in a couple of hours. I never thought she wouldn't be here!"

Dior pulled her phone out and called Milani. She didn't answer the first three times, but then she finally answered.

"Where the hell are you?" Dior asked. Before she could say anything else, they ended the call.

"What happened?" I asked anxiously.

"She's on her way."

"How do you know that for sure?"

"Cuz she's in a car."

"I hope she's on her way for real."

Twenty minutes later, the front door opened and in walked Milani... with company. I rushed over to her and hugged her tightly.

"Where have you been?" I asked. "Are you alright?"

"Don't I look alright?" she asked with a smile. "Javarius took very good care of me."

"Really Milani? You've been gone all night, and you walk in here making jokes," Dior said with an attitude.

"In case y'all haven't noticed, I'm grown! I can do whatever I want, whenever I want to and with whoever I wanna do it with!" Milani responded.

"Not as long as you're living under this roof! I won't have you running around Vegas being a thot!" Dior argued.

"Okay, let's not say something we'll regret later!" I spoke aggressively as I jumped between the two of them.

"I'm not saying nothing that I'll regret later. Mom is gone and Jaylen was nice enough to move us out here. I'm not gonna have the two of you running around this strange city..."

"Aht! Aht! Aht! You are not responsible for me Dior! I know that you're older than me and mom asked you to keep an eye on me and Imani, but you aren't responsible for me!" Milani shot.

"Then tell me something Milani... if I'm not responsible for you, who is?" Dior asked.

"My husband is!" Milani stated as she flung her left hand out.

I almost passed out when I saw the huge rock on her left ring finger. I couldn't even say anything for a couple of minutes because my tongue felt like it was attached to the roof of my mouth.

"I know that you did not marry this man!" Dior spat before I could get my damn mouth to work.

"I did."

"Oh, hell naw!" Dior shrieked as she looked at Javarius with rage in her eyes. "You married my little sister or is this some lie y'all made up so she could get away with being out all night?!"

"She's not lying. We really did go to the chapel and get married," Javarius said with an amused expression on his face.

"Uh, aren't you like in your thirties or something?" I asked.

"Thirty- two," he said with a smile.

"My sister is twenty- three years old!"

"Right, she's an adult," Javarius said politely, which I felt was his way of antagonizing me.

"You took advantage of her! Were you drinking last night Milani?" I asked.

"Okay, okay. This is not going the way I thought it would. As a matter of fact, it is going the way I expected cuz I knew this wasn't going to go well. However..."

"Milani, you can't be serious!" I interrupted.

"However! We are married now! Whether I was drunk or not last night has nothing to do with the fact that I am completely sober now! I might not know Javarius that well, but Dior is planning to marry Jaylen in the near future... even though she's only been knowing him for TWO MONTHS!!" Milani stated as she raised two fingers in the air.

"Two months is a lot longer than twenty-four hours Milani! You have known this man less than that, and you married him!" Dior argued.

"So what Dior! It's my fucking life and I can do whatever I wanna do! Look, I love y'all but I'm not gonna let y'all stress me out over this. Javarius asked me if I wanted to get the marriage annulled..."

"YES! YES, you wanna get it annulled!" Dior yelled.

"No, I don't!" Milani stated firmly.

"Milani! You cannot be serious about this marriage!" Dior argued.

"I'm as serious about our marriage as you are about marrying Jaylen! Javarius is a great guy..."

"You don't know him well enough to make that determination!" I interjected.

"I know what I need to know to try out this marriage and try to make it work," Milani said. "Now, if you both will excuse me, I'm gonna go pack my things."

"Pack your things for what, Milani?" I asked.

"To move in with my husband. How are we supposed to make our marriage work living in two different houses?" Milani inquired. "Babe I'm just gonna go get my things and I'll be right back."

She kissed Javarius on the lips before walking to the bedroom that was supposed to be ours. Of course, I followed behind her. I needed to know where her damn head was at.

"Milani are you sure about this?" I asked.

"Absolutely!"

"This is insane! You can't do this!"

"Imani, just give him a chance and let us have a chance to try and make this work. You should see his house! He lives in a huge mansion with a six- car garage!"

"Don't take this the wrong way sis, but I don't give a rat's ass! I'm worried about you!"

"Don't be! Look at me, Imani! I'm fine! Why are you and Dior making such a big deal out of this?!" she asked. "Didn't we move out here so we could find happiness?"

"How can you be happy?" I asked with concern.

"Like I am!"

"With a man you don't know!"

"I'll get to know him! Look, I didn't come here to argue with you or Dior. I just wanted you to know why I didn't come back here last night and that I'm moving out," Milani said. "If you want to, you can come with us. There's more than enough room and I'm sure Javarius wouldn't mind."

"You don't know him sis," I repeated.

"Stop saying that like it's gonna make a difference. Do you see this ring? Do you know how many racks he dropped on this?"

"I don't care!"

"Maybe not, but that means he's willing to give this marriage a real chance. So, if he's willing to do that, I'm gonna do the same," she explained.

"I just thought we were gonna share the experience of Vegas together," I said sadly.

"And we will. Just cuz I'm moving out doesn't mean I'm gonna stop being your sister,

Imani." She walked over to me and hugged me tightly. "I'm always gonna be here for you, sis. You're my best friend in the whole world. I'd never forget about you or what we share."

"But you're going to a whole new life. What if you meet new friends? Will you forget about me then?" I asked, feeling my heart breaking.

She pulled back a little and looked me dead in my eyes. "Never! I told you that you can come with me sis. Javarius would welcome you in and the place is huge, so you wouldn't be in anyone's way. He has a housekeeper and personal jeweler, and he's the sweetest person. Maybe he can hook you up with one of the guys on the team."

"I don't know sis."

"Please. I would love it if you came with me."

It didn't take me long to make a decision. I loved both my sisters, and I never imagined that I would have to choose who to live with. I just hoped I was making the right decision.

Chapter seven

Dior

When Imani told me that Milani didn't come home last night, I was livid! Where the fuck was our sister? My mom entrusted me to keep them safe and she had already left with a dude she didn't know, stayed out all night, and now she wasn't answering her damn phone!

If I wanna fuck somebody up was a person, it would be me because where the hell did that man have my little sister? When she finally walked through the door, of course, I was happy to see that she was safe, but that bubble quickly burst when she informed me and Imani that she had gotten married last night.

How the hell could she have married a man she didn't even know? He was a complete stranger, and she actually ran off and got married to him! Then she let us know that she was moving out. As soon as she disappeared into the bedroom with Imani on her heels, I laid into Javarius.

"Okay, what I need you to do is get this marriage annulled as quickly and quietly as possible!" I told him.

"What? Why would I do that?" he asked with a smug grin on his face.

"Because you don't know anything about my sister! How could you take advantage of her like that when you knew she was drunk?"

"Did Milani tell you that she was drunk? I heard her say that she was drinking. We both were, which isn't illegal since she's of legal age. I did not take advantage of your sister. She was of sound mind when she signed her name on the marriage certificate," he said.

"I don't care! You need to release her of this marriage, and I'm not playing with you!"

"Is that a threat?"

"No, but I'm coming to you as a sister. Our mom just passed away last week, so my sister is still grieving."

"I know. She told me about that, and I'm sorry for your loss. I can't possibly imagine what you're going through," he had the nerve to say.

"If you're really sorry, you would put an end to this farce of a marriage!"

"I'm not gonna do that. I made a commitment to Milani and until she tells me she doesn't want this to work, I'm gonna put forth every effort. I'm sorry you can't be happy for us for whatever reason. I've never been to jail. I don't have any kids or baby mamas floating around. And I make great money, which means I can support your sister."

"I don't care about that!"

"Then what do you care about?"

"I care about your sister," he said.

"How can you? You just met her last night!"

"Yes, and we spent the whole evening talking and getting to know each other! I know a lot more than you think I do," he responded with a smirk.

"Like what?" I asked with an attitude.

Before he could answer, the door to the bedroom opened and Milani and Imani walked out. What shocked me the most was that Imani had a suitcase too!

"What the hell is going on?" I asked.

"Imani decided that she wants to come stay with me and Javarius. Is that okay, babe?" Milani asked as she turned her attention to her husband.

"Yea, your sister is more than welcome..."

"OH, HELL NAW!" I shrieked. "Imani you can go put that suitcase away because you aren't going anywhere!"

"Please don't make this harder than it needs to be Dior," Imani said with a sad expression on her face. "I love you and I love Milani, but we all know that me and Milani have been closer than you and I. I just don't want to be here without her."

"Is it because the two of you had to share a room?" I asked.

"No. It has nothing to do with that. Milani and Javarius just met and got married. I just wanna be close by if she needs me. I may come back here. I don't know. Right now, I wanna go with Milani."

That shit hurt my feelings. It was almost like she had taken a knife and stabbed my heart then twisted it. I understood why Milani felt she had to leave. I mean, she did go ahead and marry the dude. But I thought I'd at least have Imani here with me. Now, she wanted to leave me too.

Tears slipped from my eyes as I stood there staring at my sisters. "What am I gonna do without y'all?" I asked with a frown.

"You can come visit us anytime you want to, and we'll come see you sometimes too," Imani said.

"Yea sis. We love you. We're not trying to shut you out of our lives," Milani affirmed.

The two of them wrapped their arms around me for a group hug. I wanted to bawl my eyes out, and I was probably going to do that as soon as they left. When my mom asked me to look out for my sisters, I was sure this wasn't what she had in mind.

"This is not the vision I had for us when we moved here," I cried sadly.

Milani pulled back and said, "It's not the vision I had for us either, but I'm happy about the way things are shaping up." She looked at Javarius and smiled.

He returned her smile and winked. "I promise to take good care of your sisters," he said.

"I don't want y'all to go!" I cried as I pulled them in for a hug again. "Mama made me promise that I'd look out for y'all. How can I do that if y'all move out?"

"Dior, I know you didn't expect us to live together forever," Milani said as she looked at me sideways.

"Well, not forever but we just got to Vegas. It's just too soon!" I cried.

"Would it make you feel better if you saw where we were moving to?" Imani suggested.

Shit, why didn't me or Javarius think of that? Well, maybe he had thought about it but didn't want me to know where they were going to be living. Maybe he wanted to take my sisters away from me forever. My sisters were young and naïve, so they couldn't see this shit for what it really was.

What man in his right mind introduced himself to a female and married her in the same night? That sounded like some sex trafficking shit in the making if you asked me, but of course, I couldn't say that out loud because then I would push my sisters further away from me. Lord, this was a disaster!

Had I known then what I knew now, I would have kept our asses struggling in Houston.

After a few moments of silence and all eyes on me, I replied, "Yes! I think it would make me feel better."

"Is that okay, babe?" Milani asked as she walked over to Javarius and wrapped her arms around his large frame.

He looked into her eyes and smiled before responding, "Of course."

She puckered her lips, and he pressed his against them. How the hell could they be so loving and comfortable with each other when they were still strangers? That dick must be good as hell!

"Okay, can we go now because I promised Jaylen I'd be here when he got back from work," I said as I looked at my phone for the time.

"Sure," Javarius said as he grabbed both of the girl's suitcases and we headed out the door.

I could not believe this shit was happening, but at least I would know where to start looking for my sisters if they went missing. Once we made it outside and he unlocked the doors of a Mercedes G Wagon, my mouth almost hit the ground.

"This is yours!" Imani asked excitedly.

"Yea, y'all climb in and I'll put the bags in back," Javarius suggested.

We all climbed in, and the truck smelled like it was fresh off the lot. Even though I was impressed with his choice of vehicle, it was going to take a lot more than this vehicle to get me off his ass. He shut the back and climbed in behind the wheel. Once he pushed the button to start the vehicle, backed out of the parking spot and we were on our way.

On the drive to his house, he reached over and locked fingers with Milani. She looked over and smiled at him. It was disgusting to watch. You would have sworn they had known each other for months or years instead of a damn day! Shit, it still hadn't been twenty- four hours.

Once we got into this subdivision with these humungous ass mansions, I could tell that Imani was deeply impressed. I would be lying if I said I was too because this was on a level that we had never known before. Where we came from, all we knew was low income and project housing, Section 8 and food stamps, struggle and depression. But we also knew love because our mom made sure we knew how much she loved us every day.

Love wasn't about material things, even though we were envious of some of the lifestyles our friends led. Love was about what was in the heart. However, looking around us, I had to admit that I would not mind being loved like this.

Javarius pulled into the gate of a huge estate. The driveway was long, and the property was beautiful. When he pulled up, he sucked his teeth when he saw a car in his driveway.

He didn't even bother opening the garage door. He parked right next to the car and told us to stay inside. "What's going on?" Milani asked.

"I don't know, but I need y'all to stay put and let me handle this," he said as a female stepped out of the white Honda Accord.

"I know you don't have a bunch of bitches in that truck!" the female yelled angrily.

"What the fuck are you doing here, Whitney? Matter fact, how the fuck did you find out where I lived?" Javarius asked as he stepped out of the truck.

"I've been calling and texting you all fucking night and this is what the fuck you were doing?!" she yelled. "Fucking with these random bitches!"

"Random bitch!" Milani expressed. "Oh, hell naw! That bitch needs to know that I ain't nobody's random!"

She unbuckled her seatbelt and I asked, "Where are you going?"

"To let that bitch know that whatever she had with Javarius is over and that I'm his wife! Not the random bitch that she thinks I am!" Milani fumed.

"I think you should let Javarius handle his own business," Imani said nervously.

"No, cuz he can't put hands on her like I can!" Milani snarled.

"What? You can't fight that girl! You don't even know what their relationship is!" I argued.

"I don't care! Do you see how she's putting her hands in his face? I don't like that shit! Y'all stay here cuz I don't want her to think we're trying to jump her! Trust me, I can handle this hoe all by myself!" Milani stated.

"I'm gonna call the police," I said.

"You don't even know the address!" Imani stressed.

"Stay here!" Milani ordered and hopped out of the truck.

"Oh, I know this bitch not about to step to me!" the female yelled as she glared at Milani.

It took everything in me not to get out of the truck. This was not what I was expecting to happen when I agreed to see where they would be living.

"I ain't gon be too many more bitches!" Milani stated.

"Who the fuck are you?" the woman yelled.

"Whitney can you just go? I don't know how the fuck you found out where I live, but if you come around here again, I'm gonna have you arrested for trespassing!" Javarius stated angrily.

"Arrested for trespassing! How can you say that to me after everything we meant to each other?" she whined.

"We had a lot of fun..."

"FUN! IS THAT WHAT WE'RE CALLING IT NOW?!" she hollered.

"That's all it's ever been!" Javarius stated. "I need you to leave!"

"I'm not going no fucking where until you tell me who this bitch is!" Whitney yelled. "Is she the bitch who is supposed to be replacing me?"

"If that's what you wanna call it, but she's more than you were..." he said.

"And how is that?" Whitney asked. "I hope you don't think he's gonna do anything more than fuck you and your friends..."

"First of all, those are my sisters, and second, I don't know what he did with you, and I don't care! But whatever it was is in the past!" Milani stated.

"Nah, it's not! He'll be back as soon as he's done with you, and I'll be waiting for him!" Whitney surmised.

"Well, you're gonna be waiting cuz MY HUSBAND ain't gonna contact you no more!" Milani argued as she showed off her ring.

"Tell her Milani!" Imani cheered.

"WHAT THE FUCK!! I KNOW YOU DID NOT MARRY THIS BITCH!!" the woman hollered before she started swinging punches on Javarius.

That was when Milani jumped on her and started pulling her hair and punching her face. She was swinging too, but Milani was moving on her like a wasp on a nest.

"That bitch is crazy!" I stated as me and Imani both jumped out of the truck.

There were a lot of screams and hands being thrown around, but we finally managed to separate the two of them. As Javarius held on to Whitney, he growled angrily before opening the door to her car and shoving her ass inside. As she fought to get out, he closed the door.

"I swear to God, if you don't get out of here right now, I will call the police!" he threatened.

"You can't do this to me Javarius! I love you!"

"GET THE HELL OFF MY PROPERTY WHITNEY!! AND DON'T YOU EVER COME AROUND HERE AGAIN!!" he hollered in a booming voice that had scared me too.

The woman quickly started her car and rolled down her passenger window. "This ain't over bitch!" she threatened Milani.

"Bring it bitch!" Milani countered as she showed her ring again before walking over to Javarius and putting her arms around him.

The woman put her car in drive and sped out of the driveway on two wheels. "Are you alright?" Javarius asked Milani as he checked her face for any wounds from the assault.

"I'm okay."

"You have a scratch on your face," he said. "I am so sorry about that shit, man!"

"I have to admit that this is not what I signed up for..."

"I know, and I'm sorry."

"Who is that woman?" I asked.

"How about we go inside and talk about it? I need to put some peroxide on that scratch," he said as he locked the truck, and we headed inside.

After he turned the alarm off, he said, "Y'all can make yourselves comfortable wherever. I'll be right back."

As I stared at the high ceiling in the entryway, I admired the cathedral ceiling with the huge chandelier. The marble flooring was so beautiful and exquisite.

"Come on, we can sit in here until Javarius gets back," Milani said as she led us to the kitchen.

I was extremely impressed now. The view into the backyard was amazing from the floor to ceiling windows. There was a large circular pool and hot tub, and we could see the entire Las Vegas strip from where we were. We sat at the large island on the barstools as Javarius rushed in with a bottle of peroxide and some cotton balls.

He walked over to Milani and turned the stool towards him. As he saturated the cotton ball with the medicine, he said, "That girl was a chick that I was involved with before we got married. We weren't dating but we were having sex. I was gonna let her know that we were done cuz we got married and all, but then she showed up here before I could do that."

As he spoke, he dabbed at my sister's scratches like a nurse in a hospital. He was so gentle with her and so apologetic that I almost felt bad for judging him.

"I don't know how she found out where I lived cuz I try to keep that information from the public, but when you're famous, sometimes shit like that happens," he explained.

"Do you think she'll come back?" I asked.

"Honestly, no. She's really a cool person. I ain't never seen this side of her before today..."

"How long have y'all been screwing around?" Imani asked.

"A few months."

"So, she thought y'all were in a relationship?" she surmised.

"She may have thought that, but we weren't. Look ladies, I ain't trying to say that I'm perfect. I'll never do that cuz that's making myself out to be someone I'm not. Last night when me and Milani made a split- second decision to tie the knot, it was more of a joke than anything. But when I woke up next to her this morning..."

"Oh please! Spare us the details about y'all having sex!" I expressed.

"We didn't have sex!" Milani stated, which actually shocked the shit out of me.

I just knew that was her reason behind wanting to stay with him. I thought her ass may have been dickmatized. Now that she had told me that hadn't had sex, I was wondering why she was really staying in this marriage.

"Y'all didn't?" I asked.

"No! What kind of chick do you think I am?" Milani asked.

"We had been drinking last night, and I knew that I didn't want her to wake up and think that I had taken advantage of her. I didn't even attempt to cross that line," Javarius said as Milani smiled from ear to ear.

"Well, if y'all didn't have sex, why are y'all trying to stay in this marriage?" I asked.

"I already told you why..."

"No, actually, you told me why babe. Maybe you should just tell them what you told me," Milani said.

"No, babe. When you and your other sister were in the room, I explained to your older sister why I wanted to be with you. But I will gladly repeat myself again, so your other sister can know..."

"Okay, all this sister, sister is giving me a headache!" Imani said with a smirk. "I'm Imani and this is Dior. Imani and Dior. Dior and Imani."

"Got it," Javarius said with a smile. "Anyway, would y'all like something to drink?"

"Sure. What do you have?" I inquired.

"Everything from water to juice to wine to hard liquor," he responded.

"Water will do."

He walked over to the fridge and pulled out four bottles of VOSS water. He handed each of us one and kept one for himself.

"I wanna apologize for what happened again. I did not mean..."

"Bae, it's okay," Milani said. "You aren't responsible for random bitches showing up at your house. Now, tell my sisters why you want to stay married to me."

While looking in Milani's eyes, Javarius spoke as if he was professing his love.

"I am choosing to stay married to you because there is something about you that excites the hell out of me. From the moment I saw you walk into that restaurant, I knew I wanted to be with you. The first time we kissed was like the magic those females talk about in the Disney movies. I literally felt my world shift on its axis. I know this sounds crazy cuz we just met last night, but I wanna ride this shit out with you and see where it takes us. Hell, we started off good, had a lil bumpy today, but we're still able to sit and talk like two rational adults. I think if we keep that same energy going forward, we can be successful in our marriage. I told you that my parents have been married for over thirty years. I want to experience that too... with you," Javarius said.

Milani grabbed his face and pulled it to her level and kissed him. I brushed a tear from my eyes because she did seem happy, so I was just going to have to trust her instincts and hope she made the right decision for her.

"Dior are you crying?" Imani asked as she draped her arm across my shoulder and pulled me close.

"His words were touching," I admitted as I sniffled.

Milani got off the barstool and came to stand in front of me and Imani. "I know you don't agree with how we did this marriage thing, but this is why I want to stay in this marriage. Javarius is a good guy, so I wish you would give him a chance the way I am," Milani said.

I nodded my head and said, "I will. Just please don't let me down."

"I won't," he confirmed as he came to stand behind Milani and hugged her from behind.

"Well, I gotta get going," I said as I hopped off the barstool.

"Already?" Milani inquired. "You just got here, and you haven't seen the house yet."

"Well, let me get an Uber to come pick me up and then y'all can show me the house," I suggested.

"Uber! Nah, lemme get the car service I use to come scoop you up," Javarius offered.

"Thank you."

"No problem. We're family," he said as he pulled out his phone and made the call.

"Well, show us around," I said to Milani.

"What you mean? I'm waiting for him to show me around too," she responded as we cracked up. "He didn't get the chance to earlier because he had his jeweler come by with the rings. Then he got on one knee and proposed. It was so amazing!"

"You sound like you're in love already," Imani surmised as she stared at our sister.

"Not there yet, but if he keeps treating me this way, it won't take me long."

"Are you guys gonna go on a honeymoon?" I asked.

"The driver is on his way. His name is Chet and he's already been paid and tipped," Javarius informed me.

"Thank you again."

"You're welcome. So, let's take that tour and Imani, I can show you where you'll be staying."

He locked hands with Milani, and they led us on a grand tour of this fabulous home. I had never seen anything like this in my entire life. The bedrooms were massive. Their master bedroom looked almost the same size as the apartment we once shared with our mom. This house had six bedrooms, eight bathrooms, a gourmet chef's kitchen, media room, office, gym, wine room with a bar, and a six- car garage. Don't even get me started on the backyard because it was absolutely gorgeous.

The room that Javarius chose for Imani not only had the best view of the city, but a balcony where she could relax and lounge. Shit, this was the life!

And it made me feel a lot better knowing that they were here and that he was going to be protecting them. I guess I really had misjudged Javarius and I was glad he changed the narrative.

BAM! BAM!

"What the fuck was that?" I asked.

Then we heard the sound of glass breaking. We all took off running outside, but before we made it there, Javarius went into the bedroom and came back out with a 9mm handgun.

"What the hell is that for?" I shrieked.

"I don't know what the fuck going on outside, so y'all stay here!" he said as he opened the door.

We could still hear glass breaking before he hollered about shooting someone. I didn't know what the hell was going on, so I pressed the button on the security alarm panel for the police.

"I'm going out there!" Milani stated.

"NO!" I yelled.

"Are you crazy? That is my husband!"

"Who you've known all of two seconds!" I shot back.

"I don't care if I've known him for two minutes! We promised for better or worse!" she scoffed and headed outside.

"Lord, have mercy!"

Chapter eight

Whitney Davis

I had a conversation with Javarius yesterday before he went to dinner with his teammates. We were supposed to hang out after he was done eating. So, I rented a room at the Tropicana Las Vegas Hotel because Javarius didn't like people in his business. He didn't want anyone to know that we were together yet for whatever reason. I was getting tired being his dirty little secret and was ready to tell the world that I loved that man.

I had planned on having that discussion with him last night, but he never showed up. I called and called and called, but he wouldn't pick up the damn phone. I called so many times that I exhausted myself to sleep.

When I woke up this morning, I started doing some investigating to find out where he lived. I mean, I had an idea, but wasn't a hundred percent sure. However, I was going to take a chance and go to the address that I had just to see if it was actually his place.

When I got there, I was truly impressed with this area. This was the type of shit little girls dreamt about when we were younger. I knew I had that dream so many times. To think that it might actually come true with Javarius had me excited. I walked up to the door expecting him to answer, but I should have known better.

A place as big as this needed a maid, butler, driver and nanny. At the end of the day, I hoped to be the one living here with Javarius.

When the woman came to the door, I wanted to walk right past her, but she wouldn't let me even get the tip of my shoe in the door let alone my whole damn body in the house.

"Can I help you?" she asked with a tight smile.

"I'm looking for Javarius Johnson. Is he here?" I asked as I tried to get inside the home.

She quickly stopped me from doing that and said, "No, he isn't."

"Where is he?"

"I'm not sure, but if you tell me who you are, I will inform him that you dropped by when he returns," she said.

I was not to be swayed by the help though. "Or I can just come inside and wait," I said through clenched teeth as I tried to get by again.

"Not in here," she stated firmly.

"Lady, I was invited here! Now, you can either let me in or I swear when I become Javarius Johnson's wife, the first thing I'm gonna do is fire you!"

She was a tough cookie though. "Like I said, Mr. Javarius isn't here. Now, you can come back at another time if you want to, but make no mistake about it, you are not getting in this house. So, unless you want to spend the rest of your day locked up in a Vegas jail, you need to get the hell off this property," she threatened.

"Fine!" I relented and turned on my heels to leave.

I couldn't believe that bitch was treating me this way. I couldn't wait to tell Javarius how she had acted towards me. He definitely needed to get rid of her ass because she was just rude and disrespectful. As soon as I got in the car, I dialed his number, but once again, he didn't respond.

I was sitting in my car going crazy, so I decided to take a drive and come back. Even though I hadn't spoken to Javarius since yesterday, I still expected him to be happy to see me. I stayed away for a couple of hours and had a chance to cool off, so I returned. When I got there, the woman who had answered the door earlier was leaving, so she informed me that Javarius had not gotten back yet. Instead of arguing with her, I simply drove off the property, hit a couple of blocks and returned.

I parked my car in the circular driveway facing the street so I could see when Javarius drove in. As soon as I saw the G Wagon, I got excited. He had told me he was considering getting this vehicle. He was actually stuck between the G Wagon and an H3 Hummer. I had advised him to get the G Wagon because it would make a statement about him.

That statement was class and money. He had bought the truck a couple of months ago, but still hadn't taken me for a ride. It was cool though because I could be very patient when it came to getting what I wanted. I knew that good things happened when you waited.

I was super excited to see him but then I saw that he wasn't alone. He had a bitch with him, and she was sitting in the passenger seat next to him. The first thing that came to my mind was who the hell was that bitch. It wasn't until he parked the truck that I noticed two more bitches in the back seat. I was livid!

How dare he fuck over me this way? Was this the reason he hadn't been answering my calls? Were these bitches why he hadn't bothered to call or text me back? Was he fucking these three bitches last night? If an orgy was what he wanted, he should have invited me to join him.

Even though that wasn't my cup of tea, I was willing to play my role when it came to being with Javarius and making him happy. I stepped out of my car and immediately started going off!

He kept asking me to leave, which really angered me! How dare he ask me to leave when I was the one who had been fucking him for the past six months. We were way past all that! I was beyond being a person of reason right now, especially once the bitch told me the two of them were married. I knew my ears had to be playing tricks on me.

I just knew he hadn't married this random bitch for real. I literally felt the wind get knocked out of my entire body as I stared at the gorgeous rock on her left- hand ring finger.

I couldn't believe this was happening! How could he have gotten married? I didn't even know he was engaged to anyone. He had me waiting for him in the hotel room all night last night and the whole time he was at some chapel saying 'I do' to this random ho!

Where the fuck did this bitch come from?

Her dress looked expensive, but her shoes looked like they came from Dollar Tree! All I saw after she flashed that fucking rock in my face was red and I wanted to hurt somebody! Before I could stop myself, I started swinging on Javarius.

"YOU MARRIED THAT RANDOM BITCH!!" I screamed as I hit him with blow after blow.

I knew that he would never hit me, and that was good because I was determined to take all of my frustration out on him. What I wasn't expecting was for the bitch to jump in and start fucking me up. She grabbed me by the hair and started punching me in the face and head.

That bitch may have had dollar store shoes, but those punches came straight from Mike Tyson. I was caught off guard a little and because of that, she got a few good licks on me before I started fighting back. My head was hurting so bad, but I wasn't about to go out like that.

Not long after the fight started, Javarius pulled me away from her but not before she managed to swing her foot and kick me in the face hard. For a full minute, I didn't know where the hell I was or what happened to me.

I was so dazed and confused that I couldn't even fight off Javarius when he lifted me up and dragged me to my car. He threw my ass in the front seat of my car and glared at me.

"If you don't get the fuck up outta here with all that shit, I promise you will be in jail by sunset!" he snarled.

"Why are you doing this to me?" I cried as tears spilled from my eyes.

"JUST LEAVE WHITNEY!! GET THE FUCK UP OUTTA HERE AND DON'T COME BACK!!"

I knew if he did call the police, it wouldn't take them long to get to this bougie ass area. Hell, they were probably waiting for a phone call right now. So, instead of continuing to argue a moot point, I just started my car and drove off.

My head was spinning really badly anyway, so I needed to go to the store and get some Tylenol or something. As I looked at my face in the mirror, tears sprung to my eyes. I wasn't even crying because my face looked like a sliced pig's ass. I was crying because Javarius had gotten married, and it wasn't to me.

"AAaaaarrrgghh!! WHYYYYYY?!! Why would you do this to us?!" I cried loudly.

I pulled into the Walgreens parking lot not too far from Javarius' home. Once I parked my car,

I grabbed a cap off the back seat and pulled it down to try to hide some of the bruises and scratches on my face. I headed to the aisle with first aid items and grabbed a bottle of peroxide, a bag of cotton balls and a box of gauze pads. Then as an afterthought, I picked up a box of Neosporin and Tylenol, which I had almost forgotten about.

When I got to the counter, I grabbed a bottle of water out of the cooler. The cashier took one look at me and gasped.

"Are you okay?" she asked with concern in her tone.

"Peachy," I responded with a fake smile and a smirk.

She didn't bother to say another word concerning my condition. She began to scan my items, then gave me the total. I reached in my purse and stuck my debit card in the machine. She handed me my receipt and bag and I headed out the door.

"Thank you. Have a nice day!" she called out.

I rolled my eyes and continued to walk out. Once I was back in the car, I cleaned the blood off the scratches on my face and put some Neosporin. Then I took three Tylenol pills before resting my head on the headrest for a few minutes. I needed to process everything that had just happened.

Javarius had gotten married. I didn't even know he was messing with someone else. I needed some answers and whether he wanted to or not, he needed to give them to me. I decided to go back to Javarius' house... not for trouble, but for those answers. It wasn't fair that some random bitch was about to enjoy the life that I deserved to have. I had been putting in a lot of work to become his wife, so this shit was total crap!

She hadn't put in any fucking work, so how the hell did she get to call herself wifey? I pulled up to the front of his house and saw his truck parked outside. I guess with all the action that took place earlier, he had forgotten to park it in the garage. Even better.

Now I knew exactly what I had to do. How dare he buy the truck I helped him pick out to ride some new bitch in!

Where the fuck they do that at?

I had followed this man all the way from Oakland, and this was how he did me. I went from being a super fan to his lover in a matter of months. Why would he fuck up the good thing that we had? I had tried my best not to let my emotions get the best of me, but I had failed. I would have done anything for Javarius... still would if he asked me.

But right now, he couldn't tell me shit! I was just too damn mad! I popped the trunk and took a deep breath before I stepped out of my car.

I walked around to the back and grabbed the tire iron. I walked over to Javarius' G Wagon, raised my arms and swung. All the pent- up emotions I felt were being taken out on this beautiful truck. I didn't give a fuck though!

I smashed out two windows and the backside quarter panel before Javarius rushed outside with a gun pointed at me.

"WHAT THE FUCK ARE YOU DOING?!!" he screamed angrily.

"WHAT THE FUCK DOES IT LOOK LIKE I'M DOING?!! I'M DESTROYING YOUR FUCKING TRUCK!!" I hollered back as I raised my arms again.

He cocked the hammer of his gun and said, "Whitney I swear to God, if you hit another part of my truck with that damn crowbar, I will shoot yo ass!"

I chuckled. I knew Javarius better than he knew himself. I knew he wasn't about to shoot me. He wouldn't even hit a woman, so I knew he wasn't going to fire a gun at me.

"You won't shoot me," I taunted with a smirk.

The look on his face was anything but amusing. He actually was staring at me like he didn't know me at all. That scared the hell out of me. Maybe I had taken things a little bit too far, but this wasn't my fault! This was all Javarius' fault!

If he was looking for me to take the blame for this shit, he had me fucked up. I was sure he thought that I was deranged or out of my mind though, but men did that to you sometimes.

"Swing that crowbar and you will definitely find out!" he stated as he held the gun on me.

Next thing I knew, I heard sirens, but before I had a chance to react, several police cars pulled up. I quickly dropped the tire iron to the ground and held my hands up.

"YOU CALLED THE COPS!!" I screamed. I knew I had fucked his truck up, but it was nothing that his insurance wouldn't fix.

I couldn't believe he had taken it this far and called the police on me. Surely, we could have worked this out between the two of us. How the hell could he do this to me? As the police parked their trucks and got out of the vehicles, Javarius finally put his gun away.

"What's going on here, Mr. Johnson?" asked one of the officers.

Of course, they would know who the fuck he was. And how the hell did they get here so damn fast? Like I said, they were probably riding around the area waiting for something to jump off. I knew I should have taken my ass home after me and that girl fought!

"Isn't it obvious?" his wife asked with an attitude as she made her presence known. "THAT BITCH BUSTED OUT MY MAN'S WINDOWS!!"

"Calm down babe," Javarius said. Then he turned his attention back to the police. "This woman showed up here earlier…"

"This woman! Oh, is that what we're doing now?!" I asked angrily.

"Ma'am I'm only gonna ask you to be quiet once," the officer said.

"Well, why does he get to tell his side first?" I asked in a whiny tone.

"Because I asked him to!" he replied with some bass in his tone.

Like damn! I wasn't even being rude to his ass! Everybody always catered to the ball players and said fuck the little people! I was sick and tired of that shit!

I didn't have a choice but to shut up at this point. This cop didn't look like he was down for any games or my tirades.

"Go ahead Mr. Johnson."

"I asked her to leave my property earlier after she picked a fight with me and my wife..."

"Your wife? I wasn't aware that you were married," the cop said.

"That makes two of us!" I threw in.

He shot a look in my direction that had me pinching my lips like I had a duck beak or something.

"We actually just tied the knot last night," Javarius announced as he put his arm around his wife's shoulders.

"Congratulations!!" the three officers said with smiles on their faces.

"Thank you," Javarius said with a huge smile on his face.

"So, let me guess, this is an ex, and she wasn't happy to hear about the news," the cop added as he gave his own interpretation of what happened while staring at me.

"No, she's not an ex. We were just friends," Javarius stated as he tried to downplay our relationship.

"We were not just friends, and you know it!" I snapped. The cop looked at me and I quickly apologized because I didn't want to get in any more trouble than I was already in.

"We were JUST FRIENDS!!" Javarius repeated.

"Then we must have been FRIENDS WITH BENEFITS CUZ WE SURE WERE FUCKING TIL YOU MARRIED HER!!" I shot back.

"Friends!"

"So, your friendship with her was so good that she destroyed your property?"

"That's exactly what happened."

"Okay. So, how would you like to proceed?" the cop asked.

"What the hell kinda question is that? That ho destroyed his truck! We want her ass arrested!"

his wife shrieked. "That's how WE want to proceed!"

"Babe..."

"I'm sorry but why would you not want to press charges against her after what she did? That was a crazy question!" she continued.

"Just chill. Why don't you and your sisters go inside and let me handle this?" Javarius suggested.

"I don't wanna go in the house!" his wife said with her arms crossed over her chest.

"I promise I won't be long," he promised as he kissed her with me standing right there.

What kind of shit was that? This nigga had no regards to my feelings at all!

"Come on Milani," one of her sisters said as they led her inside.

I was glad he sent her ass inside. That probably meant he was going to charge this shit to the game since it was his fault that I became unglued anyway. Maybe the police would actually let me go. On the inside, I was smiling. If they let me go, I was going to pick my tire iron up and head out.

Whether Javarius wanted to admit it or not, I knew he had feelings for me. Eventually, he would step outside of his marriage and hit me up. And when he did, I would go running because I had given up a lot to move to Vegas to follow Javarius. He had no idea what it took for me to get here.

"Mr. Johnson, what would you like us to do?" the officer asked.

"What you mean? Look at my truck! She did that shit! I want her arrested and charged for the damage she did! I just bought this whip, and because she came over here UNINVITED and found out that I got married, she decided to bring her ass back over here, take that crowbar and bust out my windows! You can also charge her ass with trespassing cuz when I sent her away earlier, I told her not to come back!"

"Javarius seriously!! YOU'RE GONNA HAVE ME PUT IN JAIL?" I questioned with pleading eyes.

"You damn right! You need to know that you can't just go around destroying people's shit every time yo ass get mad!" he replied angrily.

"Well, how did you expect me to react?"

"NOT LIKE THIS!!"

"I helped you pick that truck out..."

"You gave your fucking input! You didn't put in on this shit!"

"So! How did you think I was gonna feel when you decided to ride other bitches in it before me?!" I asked.

"Aye! Watch your mouth when you talk about my wife!" he warned.

"Okay, enough of that. Ma'am, I need you to put your hands behind your back please," the cop said.

"What? For what?" I asked nervously.

"You're under arrest ma'am for destruction of property, disturbing the peace and trespassing," the officer stated. "Now, please don't make this harder than it has to be and just put your hands behind your back."

Okay, the reality of my situation definitely slapped me in the face when he said that shit! Javarius was really going to just stand there and let this man arrest me!

"Javarius please don't do this!" I begged.

He didn't even respond as he folded his large arms over his chest. "Ma'am please put your hands behind your back. I won't ask you again. We'll just have to force the cuffs on you and charge you with resisting arrest," the cop said. "Trust me, you don't want it done that way."

At this point, I had no choice but to put my hands behind my back. Tears streamed from my eyes as I looked at Javarius for help, but he just stood there unbothered. When did he stop caring about me? And if that was really the case, why hadn't he told me anything?

After the officer slapped the cuffs on my wrists, he read me my Miranda rights. I could not believe this was happening.

"Would you like us to have your truck towed to a dealership or something?" the cop offered.

"Oh nah, nah! I got this, but you can tow her shit though!" he responded.

"JAVARIUS REALLY!! YOU HATE ME THAT MUCH!!" I cried.

One of the other officers walked over and informed us that the tow truck was on the way. "You can come by the station in a couple of days to pick up the police report, so you file a claim with your insurance company," the officer advised.

"Bet! Thank you, guys for coming so quickly," Javarius said as they shook hands.

"No problem. The tow truck is on the way. Congrats again on the marriage."

"Thanks."

After I was helped into the back seat of the patrol vehicle, Javarius stood outside and took pictures of his truck. As the police were driving off with me, a truck was pulling in. I wondered who that was. It seemed as if everybody was welcome at his place but me.

I didn't know what the hell I was going to do. I was actually being hauled off to jail. I wish I could say that was the first and last time, but circumstances kind of made that impossible for me to stay out of trouble.

Chapter nine

Javarius

One week later...

The past week had been great. Me and Milani were taking the time to get to know each other and learn whatever we could about one another. We definitely got married at the right time because it was off season for football. That gave me a lot of free time to spend with my new bride. The only thorn in my side was having Imani around.

It wasn't that I didn't like her because she was a cool chick. I just thought that as a newly married couple without any kids, having her sister around was distracting for our relationship. Lucky for me, Imani wasn't built like my wife, so there was no physical attraction to her at all.

She was pretty, but her body was lacking the shit that made me want to marry Milani after just meeting her. I still hadn't told my family about my marriage to Milani. We had been keeping a low profile so our names could stay out of the blogs until I had a chance to tell them. We had decided to invite them over tonight to break the news to them.

I had filed the claim with my insurance company to have my truck fixed, so someone from the Mercedes dealership had just come by to drop it off. I was as excited to get my ride back as I was the day I purchased it. Even though I had three other vehicles I could have used, this one had quickly become my favorite.

I walked up behind Milani as she stood in the bathroom mirror staring at her reflection. "You okay?" I inquired as I looked into her eyes through the glass.

"I'm so nervous!"

"Why?"

She turned around and wrapped her arms around me. She looked up at me and asked, "What if they don't like me?"

I lifted her up and placed her bottom on the marble countertop. "What's not to like? You're beautiful, fine, smart! Why wouldn't they like you?"

"I don't know. Maybe cuz I don't have anything to offer you. I came from the Houston projects Javarius. What if they feel I'm not good enough for you?" Milani asked sadly.

"You keep ragging on being from the projects, but ain't nothing wrong with that. You told me yourself that your mom showered you and your sisters with love..."

"She did," Milani confirmed.

"And that's what matters. It isn't gonna matter to my family where you came from. What's gonna matter to them is that you were raised to love, and even though we haven't fallen in love yet, knowing that your mom raised you that way means you're capable of loving someone. My family is gonna love you, so stop worrying."

"Are all your siblings coming?"

"As far as I know. My brother Julian and his wife won't be here until tonight though," I informed her.

"So, does that mean we're gonna wait until Julian gets here to let the family know we got married?"

"Oh, naw! We gon stick to the plan and gather them around the backyard at seven and make the announcement! Then we gon party until we get tired…"

"Or drunk," Milani finished as she burst into laughter.

"Nah, nah, nah! Ain't gon be none of that drunk stuff," I said with a chuckle. "But we are gonna have some fun."

She placed her hands on both sides of my face and kissed me. We still hadn't had sex yet, but I was not going to rush her. We had done the marriage shit backwards. We got married before we fell in love. We got married before we had sex. We got married before meeting each other's families.

I never knew I wanted to be married until I took that step with Milani. Before we said, 'I do', I thought I was out there living my best life. But over the past week being with my wife, I had come to realize that I had just started living my best life. I used to wake up to a different female, sometimes two, in a hotel room.

But waking up to my wife over the past seven days had been amazing. I wanted to be with her and make her happy. I just wanted us to stay on this path because I knew if we did, it would take us to places we had never been before.

We still hadn't gone on a honeymoon, but I had something planned for us. I just wanted to wait until our families knew about us. The last thing I wanted was for my parents to find out about my marriage from television or blogs. Believe it or not, my parents knew their way around the internet.

"You better stop before I'm unable to stop myself," I said as I hugged my wife.

"Do you have any regrets about how we tied the knot?" Milani asked.

"No indeed. Shit, I wish we had met and done this two years ago! That way, I would've had you knocked up by now!" I stated as I laughed.

"Ooooohhh, I see. So, your goal is to get in there and knock me up, huh?" she teased.

"Nah. Well, eventually," I admitted as I blushed. "But for right now, I just wanna enjoy us. I wanna travel with you and do things with my wife that I ain't never did with no female before."

"I like the sound of that."

"Come on. Let's get dressed before everyone starts getting here. You wearing the white dress I bought you, right?"

"Yea, I'll wear it. You gon have me out here looking like a bride," she said as her cheeks turned red.

"You are a bride. My bride!"

"And I'm happy about that."

I looked deep into her eyes and asked, "Are you really?"

"Yea. I mean, I thought I would be a little wild out here in Vegas for a while, but you snatched me up," she said with a smile.

"Shit, I'm glad I did. If I wouldn't have, someone else might have. Then I would have been looking from the sidelines wishing I had said something at the restaurant."

"I'm glad you said something too. I didn't realize how much I wanted to be in a relationship 'til I met you." Her eyes became glassy as she looked down.

I tilted her chin upwards so she could look into my eyes. "Don't do that. I want you to always look into my eyes when you speak to me... even when you're crying."

"Why are you so good to me?"

"Cuz I want this. I want you, and I wanna learn to love you," I admitted.

"Why me though? You could have any woman that you want. Why did you choose me?"

"There was just something about you. Something drew me to you the moment I saw you walk in that restaurant. I knew that you were the one," I confessed.

"I don't have a job. I don't have a penny to my name..."

"Babe, shush! We already discussed that, and I told you what's mine is yours."

"And I told you that I don't want to feel like I married you for your money or what you can do for me," she said for the fiftieth time since she moved in.

"Look, I know you ain't marry me for my money. In my heart, I know that shit. You ain't married me for my sex game either. For whatever reason we got married, we are here now. You respect me and I respect you. We have a mutual understanding of where we want this to go. The biggest thing between us right now is trust, and I trust the hell out of you until you give me a reason not to. So, for the last time, what is mine belongs to you. Matter of fact." I left her sitting on the counter and went to the room.

"Where are you going?" she asked.

"Just hold up nah," I said.

I went into the drawer of the nightstand on my side of the bed and pulled out the plastic with my wife's name on it. I rushed back to the bathroom holding it behind my back.

"What do you have there?"

"This is for you," I said as I handed her the card.

"What the hell!"

"Shit, you're a Johnson now baby. This is your own card to OUR bank account. I won't get into the issue of finances and how much is in there, but know that if I wanted to, I could purchase an island if I wanted to. God has blessed me with way more than the football league because he guided me towards my investments, and shit has worked out way better than I could have ever imagined. Like I could quit playing football today, and I would be good. We would be good. I know y'all struggled when y'all were growing up, but that part of your life is over. You never have to face another struggle again... not as long as I'm around," I promised.

Tears were streaming from her eyes as she wrapped her arms around my neck and hugged me tightly. I didn't even know that I was crying until I looked at my reflection in the mirror and saw tears in my eyes.

She pulled back and pressed her lips on mine. It didn't take long for my tongue to find its way into her mouth. When she reached for the bottom of my shirt and pulled it off, I was a bit taken aback. She and I hadn't taken things this far before.

She kissed me again before she reached for my shorts and unbuttoned it. That was when I pulled back because I didn't want her to start something she couldn't finish. This was the furthest we had gotten since we decided to stay married.

"Are you sure about this?"

"Don't you want to?" she asked with a look of uncertainty on her face.

"Oh, hell yea, I want to!"

"Then stop talking," she said and stuffed her tongue in my mouth again.

I unbuttoned the buttons on her shirt even though I wanted to rip that shit off her. As I pulled back and looked at her beautiful skin, I removed her bra. Her big boobs sat high and perky on her chest. I just wanted to suck on them and that was exactly what I did.

I cupped both of them in each hand and flicked my tongue along her nipples. She moaned deeply as she held my head in place. I wrapped my lips around her right boob and sucked on it.

Those titties was nice and all, but I was trying to get to that kitty cat. "You ready to take this all the way?" I asked.

"As far as you wanna go," she flirted as she slipped her hand in my boxers. "Oooohhh shit! Zaddy workin' with a monsta!"

"You damn right I am!"

"Then I'm really trying to go THAT far!" Milani admitted as she kissed me while stroking my dick.

Hell, she ain't said but a word!

I immediately pulled her shorts off as well as her small ass panty. After tossing them both to the side, I dropped down to my knees and pulled her body closer to the edge of the counter. I hadn't eaten pussy before, but I watched enough porn to know how to do it the correct way.

I would be lying if I said females hadn't sucked my dick before, but I wasn't about to be giving head to just anybody. Milani was different though... she was my wife!

I knew for a fact that my dad wouldn't be going around licking anybody's cat, and he had raised me right. I had tried my best to respect women because I had two sisters, and I wouldn't want a dude disrespecting them.

As I slid my tongue through the sweet folds of my wife's yoni, she moaned softly. I latched my lips around her clit and sucked on it. Her body tensed as it began to quiver.

Damn! I must be doing something right for her to be creaming that fast!

I continued to drive my tongue up and down the sweet center of her treasure box. I sucked and licked until she begged me to stop. Several minutes later, I stood up and dropped my bottoms on the floor. As I stepped out of them, I reached in the drawer for a condom.

"You keep condoms in your bathroom drawer?" she inquired with a puzzled expression.

"Oh, make no mistake about it, I just bought these. Matter of fact, Evita got them for me. I can show you the receipt," I explained. "Ain't no woman ever been in here before you except for Evita and my family. Period!"

"Oh kay," she said. "I believe you."

I strapped up and pulled her close to me. As I stuffed my tongue in her mouth, I stuffed my sausage in her burrito. She held on to me as I thrust in and out of her tight pussy.

"Aaaahhh!" she moaned against my lips.

As the intensity for me to pleasure her grew, I lifted her ass off the counter and held her tightly while driving that dick deep into her.

"Oh... my... gawd!" she moaned breathlessly.

Those were my sentiments exactly! Milani's pussy was so tight, it made me wonder if she was a virgin. I couldn't have been the only one to hit it though because it would have been painful. She was enjoying this dick too much to say one had never entered before. But I wasn't going to worry about that because I had a past too.

Milani wasn't the first woman I had been with in my life, and she knew that. If I could spare her from hearing about those wild times since I signed with the NFL, I would but I knew she would eventually find out. But like me, she didn't care about my past because I didn't have any children out there or any disrespectful baby mamas that she would have to deal with.

As my dick buried deep inside her pussy, we were both moaning like wounded sheep in that bathroom. I wanted to make love to my wife the right way though, so after holding her in my arms for a few, I walked out of the bathroom and into the bedroom.

As I laid her on the bed, I kissed her with all the passion that I had built up inside me over the past week. Sleeping next to this gorgeous woman without making love to her had been murder on my dick. You ever wanted to eat a piece of cake that was staring you dead in the face, but you couldn't touch it? That was how I had been feeling sleeping with Milani the past seven days!

I raised her right leg on my shoulder and pounded her cat. "Aww damn!" she moaned. "Sssshhhiiit!"

"Feels good?"

"Uhm hm!"

We continued to pleasure each other until I couldn't hold back anymore. As I pushed deep inside her and against her G-spot, her body shook with the amazing sensations that were running through it. Shit, I knew the feeling because I was going through it too.

After our bodies stopped shaking, I pressed my lips to hers and pulled out. I went to the bathroom to rid myself of the soiled condom. I tossed it in the trash and washed my hands. I rushed back to the bed still naked with my dick swinging.

I climbed in next to Milani and hugged her tight. I laid my head on her breasts as she lightly stroked my head with her fingers.

"I could get used to this," I said as I snuggled closer.

KNOCK! KNOCK! KNOCK!

"Yeah!" I called out.

"What time are you guys gonna come out?" Imani asked. "It's almost 5:30 and Javarius' family is supposed to arrive at six, right?"

"Oh shit!" I snapped. "Aight! We'll be out in a few!"

We both jumped out of bed, and I ran into the bathroom to start the shower. "I did mean for time to get away from us like that!" Milani apologized.

I stopped moving and reached for her. "I don't care about the time babe. We just shared a moment, and I have no regrets about that. So what if my family arrives and we ain't ready yet. We're newlyweds, so they will understand."

I kissed her lips and smiled. I stepped in the shower, and she followed behind me. I paused and looked at her.

"What?" She laughed. "I mean, we just had sex, so surely you don't mind taking a shower with your wife."

"Hell nah, I don't mind! The problem is my dick getting hard again," I flirted as I turned around for her to see.

"Oh, no sir! You better put that firearm away until later," she surmised.

"Ooooohhhh! Later huh?" I flirted as I walked over to her.

"Stop it, J! We have to get ready."

"I know. I know. Just have it on your mind later. This that 'to be continued' type shit!" I joked as I kissed her. "Damn, you sexy as fuck!"

"Stop it!" She blushed profusely.

My wife was definitely a bombshell. Her body was built like one of those old school Coke bottles. I was talking like PING! POW! POOM!

She really had it going on. Even though she was only twenty- three, I liked that her body and hair were natural. She had everything women paid plastic surgeons for. Her sister Imani was cute, but if she got some of her shit toned by a surgeon, she would be just as fine as Milani. Well, maybe not as fine, but she'd be aight.

I didn't think they had anyone finer than my baby. She was the ultimate woman, and she was all mine!

Chapter ten

Milani

Today was going to be a good day. That was what I kept telling myself from the moment I opened my eyes this morning. We were having a dinner party to tell Javarius' family that we had gotten married. As nervous as I was about if they would be accepting of me or not, I tried to believe that my husband knew his family better than anyone. He should know whether they would open their hearts to me or not.

I was just praying he knew his people as well as he thought he did. I was about to get ready to take a shower and get dressed, but my reflection in the mirror caught my attention. As I stared at myself, I began to feel a little anxious about meeting Javarius' parents and siblings. We had only known each other for seven days, so I wondered if his family would think I was some gold digger who married him for money.

Even though I was grateful for the money he had and the fact that he offered to take care of me, I still didn't want them to think I married him for that reason. To be honest, I barely remembered saying 'I do', but I wasn't going to confess that shit to his family. Javarius knew though because he actually carried me back to the room after the ceremony was over.

That in itself spoke volumes. And while I appreciated him giving me the option to get the marriage annulled, after listening to his reasons about why we should stay married, I agreed. I had to admit that I was intrigued by this handsome man.

Why would he want to marry a stranger when he had so many women around him that he could have married before me? But I wasn't going to focus on why he chose me. I was just going to be happy that he did.

Having sex with my husband was the last thing I expected us to do, but when he walked up to me and stood behind me, I felt something for him. When he placed me on the counter and spoke to me with so much love, I felt every word in my soul. How could I not want to give him some kitty after I heard everything he had said to me?

I did not know he was working with that monsta! He was not the first person I had slept with... he was the third, but it felt like he was the first. My kitty wasn't used to a dick of that magnitude. He had length and girth, but I kind of expected that because he was 6'5 and weighed two-hundred and fifty pounds. Compared to my 5'7, one- hundred- and- fifty pounds frame, I think that was what attracted me to him the most.

He was like a gentle giant, especially when it came to me. I didn't know how he treated other women before me, and I didn't care because they were his past and I was his present and future.

After we were done enjoying each other, I was ready to relax and hold one another. If it hadn't been for Imani, we might have fallen asleep.

My boo had worn me out and I needed a nap, but we couldn't take one.

When Javarius turned on the shower, I decided to get in with him. I mean, we had finally gotten sexual, so taking a shower was definitely a sexy thing I wanted to do. However, when I saw that his dick had gotten hard again, I had to back away. His family and my sister Dior would be here any minute now, so the last thing I wanted was for us to get into another entanglement that would make us late.

After we finished soaping ourselves, we rinsed off under the huge separate showerheads. Then we stepped out onto the huge bath rug and dried off. I wrapped the towel around my body and headed to the huge walk- in closet. I already had the white dress hanging front and center. I chose to wear a white lace bra and panty set from Victoria's Secret and after I put it on, Javarius walked up behind me and rubbed against me.

"Damn! Can ya man get a quickie?" he proposed as he rubbed his hands up and down my body.

"You better quit!" I laughed as I gently pushed him off me. "We need to hurry up..."

"C'mon bae. It ain't gon take..."

DING DONG! DING DONG!

"Aw snap!" he stated as he rushed around trying to get himself together.

"Now, you know your family does not know my sister!" I quipped.

"What that mean?"

"To have her let them in!"

"She ain't gotta let them in! Evita here!"

"She is?"

"Duh bae! We having a party! Evita is here, Chef Michael is here, and I have a few servers too."

"Damn!" I squawked. "I had no idea you had made all these arrangements. When did you do all that?"

"I've been making plans behind your back all week. I wanted to surprise you. I even hired a party planner."

"What? What did you need her to do?"

"You'll see," he said.

"Well, now I'm anxious!" I expressed happily as I slipped into my dress.

The dress was short, fitted and had spaghetti straps. The top part was covered in feathers, but it wasn't like birdy shit. It was actually very cute.

"I can't believe you really picked this out by yourself..."

"Well, I had help from Imani. She chose the dress and shoes. I just paid for it."

"Well, I appreciate you for that," I admitted as I puckered up for a kiss.

I had never heard of the designer for these shoes, but the price tag was four hundred dollars. I never had anything this expensive on my feet. I guess I had better get used to it because my hubby wanted me to enjoy the finer things he had to offer me.

After I finished getting dressed, I looked over at my handsome husband in his white Burberry shirt and white Polo shorts. He slipped his feet in a pair of white Burberry sneakers and splashed some cologne on himself.

"You ready?" he asked.

"As ready as I'll ever be," I admitted as I inhaled deeply.

He reached for my hand, and I slipped it in his. He unlocked and opened the bedroom door. As we made our way to the front, I could hear music, laughing and talking. I was shocked to see how nice it looked... not that it didn't always look nice, but I could tell someone had decorated and set the tone for a party.

Everyone was outside, so when we stepped out there, Javarius' family came rushing over to hug him. It was almost like they hadn't seen him in years. As they wrapped their arms around him, I stood off to the side and smiled. My two sisters and Jaylen came up to me and hugged me.

"You look great!" Dior complimented me.

"Thank you! Y'all look good too!" I admitted. "Hey Jaylen. Nice to see you again."

"Nice to see you. You definitely upgraded from my penthouse," Jaylen said as he looked around at Javarius' house. "Y'all have the best view of the strip!"

"Hell yea!" Imani agreed. "Some nights, I sit on my balcony and just look at the lights and action going on down there."

"The view is definitely gorgeous!" I agreed.

"Babe," Javarius said as he reached for me.

"Excuse me y'all," I told my sisters and Jaylen. I turned my attention to Javarius and his family as he wrapped his left arm around my waist.

"Mom, Dad, siblings, this is Milani," Javarius said with a smile.

"I knew you been under a female!" one of his brothers said.

"Nah, nah!" Javarius denied with a laugh. "This one is special. She ain't like any of the ones before her."

"What makes her different than the rest?" one of his sisters asked.

"Show them what makes you different, baby," Javarius encouraged.

"You just want me to..."

"I want you to show them why you're different than the other females I was messing with," Javarius said with a wink.

"What is going on?" his mom asked.

I lifted my left hand and showed my ring. Every single one of their mouths dropped as they looked from one to the other before staring back at me and Javarius.

"So, you two got married?" one of his sisters asked with a confused look on her face.

Javarius pulled his left hand out and showed his ring finger. "So, this is legit?" one of his brothers asked.

"Yea, it's legit!" Javarius confirmed. "So, Milani this is my mom Joyce, my dad Jeff, my younger sister Johnnique, my other sister Jerrika, my younger brother Josiah, and my older brother Jordy. This is your family now!"

"Welcome to the family," his mom said as she opened her arms to hug me.

"Thank you so much!" I said as I allowed her to embrace me. "I like how y'all gave all your kids names that start with J. That's so cool."

"Thank you. I have another son who was born before Jordy named Jeffery Junior. We just call him JJ," his mom said. "He'll be here a lil later."

The rest of the family hugged me and welcomed me to their family. I turned to my sisters and made the introductions. The vibe was amazing, and everyone seemed to be happy for us. That made me even more excited and hopeful for our future. The good thing was that I hadn't seen or heard from that crazy ass chick that had busted out the windows on the G Wagon. She had been trolling my social media pages though.

"Come on y'all, let's eat!" Javarius said.

We all sat down around the huge table under the white tent. I couldn't believe that my husband had put all this together behind my back. It was nice to know that he could do these kinds of things all by himself though. From what I could tell, Javarius was a great guy.

After meeting his family, I could see why he was the man that he was. While we sat down eating, I noticed there was some tension between Dior and Jaylen. What the hell was going on with them?

"So, Milani, have you met the other football wives yet?" Jerrika asked.

"No."

"Lord, wait until you meet their asses! They are some characters!" Johnnique informed me.

"They aren't that bad," Javarius said.

"Oh please bro. Some of them are ratchet as hell and they all bougie as fff..."

"Uh uh!" Mrs. Joyce cut her off with a stern expression on her face. "Ain't gon be none of that cursing at this table! Not tonight!"

"Sorry ma," Jerrika apologized quickly.

We had a great time, especially after JJ arrived with his family and Javarius' siblings started sharing stories about when they were kids. I really enjoyed listening to and learning more about my husband and his family. By the time they left, it was well after one in the morning.

Dior and Jaylen left at ten and they didn't seem to be on good terms. I vowed to check on her the next day because it was too early for them to be tripping like that. They weren't even married yet. After I said goodnight to Imani, me and Javarius turned in for the night.

"That went well," I said.

"I told you it would baby," he said.

He turned the water on in the shower and invited me to join him. Of course, I was going to get in the shower with him and this time, I wasn't going to turn him away when he reached for me. And I sure did not!

This was the perfect way to end an amazing night!

Two weeks later...

Over the past couple of weeks, me and Javarius had been all over the blogs. I wished they would just stop following me when I went somewhere. A couple of bloggers got pictures of me and my sister shopping and posted some bullshit about how I was just using Javarius for his money. They said there was no way I could have been his secret because he was sleeping with other women before we got married.

I hated that they thought that of me. I wasn't that person who they were portraying I was to the public. I used to read the comments when I saw a picture of us on The Shade Room or something, but I stopped. While some of them were positive and wishing us well with our marriage, some were extremely negative and talking shit.

So, me and my sister were out one day shopping and that dumb bitch who came to the house that day walked in the store. Imani immediately became nervous and suggested that we leave. But I was not going to do that. I mean, why should we leave when we hadn't done anything wrong? If we walked out now, it would be like she won. I refused to give her the satisfaction of thinking she ran us off.

"Uh, before this shit goes too far, maybe we should just pay for the things we have and head out," Imani suggested.

"The fuck! You're kidding right?" I gawked. I almost choked on my damn spit because she made that stupid suggestion.

"Does it look like I'm kidding? We didn't come here for trouble, and I feel like she's gonna start some."

"Then let her!" I spoke through clenched teeth. "I'm the wife! He chose me! She probably can't even afford shit in this boutique! Matter of fact, how the hell did she even know that we were here?"

"And that's why we should leave! What if she's tracking you?" Imani asked.

"She ain't that smart!" I clowned as we busted out laughing. "I'm not leaving until I'm ready to! We were here first! Why should we have to leave because that heffa walked in?!"

I didn't know what made her decide to bring her old, dry as cornbread ass over to where we were, but she did. The way she came over, I knew she wanted some smoke, and as much as I didn't want to give it to her, I was going to try and keep it classy. But don't get it twisted... if the bitch came out of pocket, she could surely get it.

"What y'all over here talking about? I know it better not be me!" she stated.

"Girl bye! Ain't nobody got time to be worried about your fucking ass!" I snapped as I proceeded to head for another clothing rack.

"Bitch don't turn your back on me when I'm talking to you!" she snapped back.

"Heffa look, maybe we got off on the wrong foot," I clowned as I turned to face her. "Cuz this shit ain't even have to go this far. You don't know me. I don't know you. What I do know is that I married Javarius Johnson and once you found out, you came unglued. But we can put that behind us and start over, so hi, my name is Milani Johnson, but you can call me Mrs. Javarius Johnson if you want to."

I stuck my left hand out for her to shake and all of a sudden, she started calling me all kinds of bitches and hoes and homewrecker. This bitch really looked like she had turned into the Tasmanian Devil from the *Loony Toons*. It was almost hilarious.

"Damn! This really how you doing it huh? In this bougie ass store!"

"Bitch, fuck you!" Whitney spat angrily.

"Why the hell are you even mad at her?" Imani asked. "Are you really that mad cuz Javarius didn't choose you? All the men they have in this city... hell, in the damn world, and you're sweating a man who wants nothing to do with you! It's just crazy!"

"Bitch, fuck you, and you can see your way out of this conversation! Nobody was even talking to yo ass!" Whitney snapped at Imani.

"Don't come at my sister like that! She ain't got shit to do with this!" I barked. "Hell, I don't even know why I have shit to do with this!"

"You inserted yourself in some shit that didn't involve you bitch! That's how the fuck you in it!"

"He's my HUSBAND!! You put your hands on him, so I put mine on you! You mad cuz he married me! Well, get over it cuz I ain't going nowhere! My husband made his choice! I don't understand why it's so damn hard for you to move the fuck on!"

"Ma'am, I'm going to have to ask you to leave," the salesperson said to Whitney.

"BITCH MAKE ME!!" she barked at the woman.

"If you don't leave, I will be forced to call law enforcement," she threatened in her bougie tone. "As for you bitch..." She turned her attention back to me and snaked her neck. "If you think I'm just gonna walk away and let you have the man that I've been grooming myself to marry one day, forget it! I can tell that you only married him to use him..."

"NOT TRUE!"

"Bullshit! I KNOW you're using him, and when he realizes that shit, he gon divorce you and come back to me!"

"Damn! That's some crazy shit! You are really so desperate that you would wait for a married man to leave his wife!" I snapped as me and Imani laughed. "Well, guess what! He already told me that he don't want you! He said he ain't never wanted you! He was just sleeping with you to past the time!" I could tell that she was getting really upset. My hope was that she'd get so pissed she would walk out of the store. I leaned in and whispered, "And I heard your coochie stank!"

Of course, I hadn't heard that, but at this point, I was going to say anything to get under her skin, so she could get the hell out of my face. All I wanted was to enjoy a peaceful afternoon of shopping with my sister... PERIOD!

My plan definitely worked. It worked so good that the bitch started to swing at me. Well, that was way more than I wanted, but I was going to defend myself. I prayed that Imani wouldn't jump in because the last thing I wanted was for anyone to think that me and my sister had jumped this crazy fool. The two of us got to tussling and fighting and then I heard the sirens.

The police came rushing through the door and separated us. "I WILL KICK YOUR ASS BITCH!!" Whitney hollered. "FUUUCK!! LET ME GO!!"

Apparently, she hadn't realized that the police were the ones holding her back. "I don't think so, ma'am. You're being placed under arrest," the cop informed her.

"UNDER ARREST!! WHAT FOR?!!" Whitney hollered.

"Assault, for one and disorderly conduct!" The officer slapped the cuffs on Whitney before turning his attention to me. "Are you alright, Mrs. Johnson."

"NO!" I fumed as I glared at Whitney.

"Do you mind telling me what happened here?" the officer asked.

"Me and my sister were in this store shopping and minding our own business when that heffa busted in here and attacked me!" I explained in true dramatic diva fashion.

"You hit me first bitch!" Whitney lied.

"No, she didn't!" Imani yelled as she showed her iPhone to the officer. "I recorded everything."

"She's right officer," said the salesperson. "And she was asked to leave but she refused."

"So, now you have a trespassing charge added to the list," the officer stated.

"Well, why not charge me for breathing while you're at it!" Whitney argued.

"You said you had a video," the officer said to Imani.

"Yes, right here," Imani responded and handed him the phone.

After the officer watched the video, he turned to look at me. "Do you might wanna let the paramedics check you out," he advised.

"THAT'S IT?! YOU'RE GONNA ARREST ME, BUT NOT HER!!"

"Ma'am you instigated this entire altercation," the officer stated with a firm expression on his face. "Had you not hit this woman, none of this would have happened. You could have just left the store like the woman asked you to."

"WOOOOOOW!" Whitney expressed angrily. "So, I'm getting arrested again and once AGAIN, this bitch gets to ride off into the sunset with MY MAN!!"

"He's not your man!" I argued as I flashed my ring once again.

"Ma'am you have the right to remain silent..."

"This shit is crazy!" she hollered.

"Anything you say can and will be used against you in a court of law..." The officer continued to read her those Miranda rights as he escorted her out of the building.

"Mrs. Johnson, I am so sorry about that," the salesperson said.

"It's cool. It's not your fault," I said.

"I know, but I can assure you that this type of behavior is not tolerated in our establishment," she continued.

"No problem. I think I'll just pay for these items and take my ass home!" I expressed.

"Yes ma'am."

She totaled up the merchandise while the other employee placed them in bags. Once I finished paying, me and Imani left the store and headed back home. I was shopping for some clothes because my husband said he was going to take me on a trip to Jamaica for our belated honeymoon. I was super excited about that especially since I had never been outside of the United States.

Hell, the first time I left Houston was to come to Vegas. Now, he was taking me to Jamaica!

"Are you excited about Jamaica?" Imani asked as we headed back home.

We were riding in Javarius' powder white Lexus IS 500. He told me that this car was a year old, but it smelled brand- new. It was as clean and shiny on the inside as it was on the outside.

"I am excited! I just am nervous now cuz I don't know what Javarius is gonna say about me fighting," I said.

"What do you mean? He shouldn't have a problem with it cuz you were defending yourself. I can show him the video and everything."

"I don't know. I just don't want him to think I'm not trying to change to be the woman he needs me to be."

"So, you wanna be one of those stuck- up, bougie bitches?" Imani asked as she turned her nose up.

"No! I don't wanna be one of them, but I'm gonna have to change my ways to be classier. I have to fit in this society that my husband belongs to, and I can't do that by wilin' like I don't have the good sense God gave me!"

"Girl bye! You act like you're ratchet or something!"

"Maybe not ratchet, but definitely not classy like those other basketball wives!"

"Those heffas been doing that shit a lot longer than you have. I think Javarius should be happy you aren't out here acting like those other hood chicks from our old projects!" Imani clowned. "Remember Penelope with the funky cat! Can you imagine if Javarius had to introduce her as his wife?"

"Girl! That's crazy!" I agreed. "I don't even wanna imagine Javarius being married to someone else."

"I know you don't and lucky for you, y'all are married and he ain't going nowhere."

"This football life is something I hadn't thought about. What if I'm not good enough to be part of the "Wives Club"? Then what?"

"What do you mean not good enough? You mean not bougie enough?" Imani asked.

"I don't know if it's just bougie. We're from the hood sis. Now, I married an NFL baller and my whole life has been turned upside down..."

"But for the better. Javarius is a great buy and he's offering you the lifestyle that we always dreamt about."

"I know. I just never imagined it would happen so fast. Last month, we were in the projects watching our mom waste away. Now look at us. Living in a multi- million- dollar mansion with housekeepers and a pool guy, car service and private chefs. Never in my life did I think this was possible."

"I know. I'll work it out."

"Maybe you're prejudging the group. Once you get to know those ladies, maybe things will change for you. Maybe they'll be more accepting than you think," Imani encouraged.

"I hope so."

"When will you meet them all?"

"Javarius said when we get back from the honeymoon, he'll have some kind of wedding reception and invite all his teammates, coaches and their wives to introduce me," I explained.

"That's pretty cool."

"Yea. So, what are you gonna do for ten days while we're gone?"

"Throw a house party, invite some men over and get busy," she said as she busted out laughing. The look I shot her way must have spoken volumes because she quickly changed her tune. "I was just kidding!"

"Uh huh!"

"Come on! You can't possibly think I was serious! As shy as I am!" Imani stated.

"So, what do you plan on doing?" I asked again.

"I'll probably go spend some time with Dior at the penthouse. I don't wanna be alone in this big ass house for ten days."

"You scared?" I teased.

"Scared of what? That stalker! No, not at all!" she responded with sarcasm.

"You think she's a stalker!" I gawked.

"How else would she have known to show up at that boutique earlier? She had to be stalking you!"

I didn't want to admit that the girl was so completely unglued, but now that Imani had mentioned it, how did she just happen to show up at the boutique at the same time we were there?

"It does explain how she knew we were there," I reasoned.

"I'm telling you, that girl is stalking you! I wonder if she's dangerous! She could be some crazy fan who had a hidden agenda to marry Javarius. I wonder if she has a psychiatric history."

"I don't think so. Now, you're overthinking," I responded with a chuckle.

"Okay, just be careful. The last thing I want is for something to happen to you."

"I'm not scared of her!"

"I know you're not. I just want you to always be aware of your surroundings."

"I will sis."

I pulled into the garage and closed the door quickly. "Uh, what about the bags in the trunk?" Imani asked with a puzzled expression.

"What you mean? We can still get them out," I said as I popped the trunk and went to grab the bags. She cracked up laughing which caused me to stare at her with a puzzling expression. "See!"

"It's okay to say you're scared," Imani said.

"I'm not," I repeated.

"Oh okay," she said sarcastically as we walked into the house.

Later that night, while me and my husband sat in bed, he turned to me and said, "I didn't wanna say nothing in front of Imani, but I need to know what happened at that boutique babe."

"Hold up," I said.

I sent Imani a text message...

Me: Please send me the video of what happened earlier

Imani: Why? Is Javarius ragging on you about it?

Me: No, nothing like that. I just wanna show him what went down

Imani: Okay

A couple of minutes later, the ding came in letting me know that the video had come through.

"Here you go," I said and handed the phone to him.

As he sat and watched the video, I could see the perplexed expression on his face. He handed the phone back to me and shook his head. "This shit is crazy! I'm sorry you had to deal with that babe," he said as he placed his arm around me and pulled me close.

"I just want you to know that I never wanted to fight that girl, especially not in a public place.

I'm trying to fit in with these rich and bougie wives and bringing the ghetto to their country club ain't gon cut it," I said.

"Well, it wasn't your fault. You were acting in self- defense."

"Yea, but I bet other people don't feel that way. They're already thinking that I married you for money."

"But we both know differently," Javarius said. "Are you looking forward to the honeymoon?"

"Yes, I am. You know I've never been anywhere," I admitted with a giggle.

"I wanna take you everywhere."

"Everywhere?"

"Everywhere."

"Like where?"

"I've always wanted to go to the Virgin Islands, the Bahamas, Hawaii, Dominican Republic, Paris, Morocco, the list goes on," he said with a huge smile.

"Well, that is quite a list." I chuckled.

"I know. And now that we're married, I can't wait to travel to all of those places with you," he said. "For right now, let me show you how much I missed you today."

"Then show me, zaddy!"

And that was how we spent the night... making love without any more talk of Whitney's crazy ass!

Chapter eleven

Dior

The past couple of weeks had been a whirlwind of activity! I was now Mrs. Jaylen McClain, wife of Dr. McClain. Now that my sisters had moved out of the penthouse, it was just me and Jaylen. With him being gone all day at work, I was kind of lonely. Even though we had only been married a week, I wondered if it was too soon to discuss us starting a family.

Since things seemed to be going really well with Milani and Javarius, maybe it was time for me to talk to Jaylen about our future. I went online to see what had been going on today. I saw a video that was titled, 'Girls Gone Wild in Clothing Boutique'.

Something told me to click on it, especially when I saw something about 'wife of Raiders defensive lineman' in the headline. I was curious to find out which football player's wife had gotten caught up in some mess. When I clicked on the video and saw my sister Milani engaged in an argument with that crazy chick that busted out the windows of Javarius' G Wagon, I rolled my eyes. I didn't even finish watching the video before I called Milani to check on her.

"Hey sis," she answered.

"What the hell happened?"

"Are you talking about that video?"

"Of course, I'm talking about that video!"

"Well, you must have seen what happened. That crazy girl came into the store talking shit. She swung on me, and I whooped her ass!" she explained.

"I can't believe that shit! How did she know where you were?" I asked.

"I don't know girl! Imani thinks she's been stalking me."

"What do you think?"

"I don't know what to think. All I know is that one minute me and Imani were shopping for clothes, and the next minute, I was fighting with that damn girl!"

"Well, I'm glad her ass got arrested... again! Something is definitely wrong with her for her to keep coming at you like that!"

"Right! I don't know what's wrong with her!"

"I do. She's desperate. Has to be for her to be chasing after him like she is when he clearly doesn't want her," I surmised.

"Well, hopefully, she will think twice before she attempts to come for me again. I mean, this is her second arrest..."

"That we know of. Have you thought about investigating her? I mean, who knows how many times she's been arrested? For all we know, she might be a repeat offender," I stated.

"This whole situation is crazy as hell. I had no idea getting married would cause so much drama. Anyway, how's your marriage going? I still can't believe you married a doctor," Milani said.

"I know right! You married an NFL player, and I married a doctor! All we had to do is get Imani married off to someone worthy of her," I said.

"Speaking of Imani, she said she was going to spend some time with you while me and Javarius went on our honeymoon. Did she talk to you about that?"

"Yea, she asked if it was okay. Of course, I said yes cuz I could use the company. When Jaylen is at work, I'm all by myself. So, it'll be nice to have someone to talk to and hang with during the day."

"That's good."

"Are you excited about going to Jamaica?" I asked.

"I can't even describe how excited I am. You know we've never been anywhere outside of Houston except here. This whole move to Vegas has been wild as hell so far. I mean, first I met and married Javarius. Then you and Jaylen tied the knot."

"And don't forget about psycho girl," I reminded her even though I was sure she hadn't forgotten.

I mean, how could she when she had just gotten into a fight with that lunatic earlier today.

"How the hell can I forget about her? That heffa is trying to turn my world upside down but I won't let her."

"I don't blame you. I know I was a bit of a skeptic when you and Javarius first got married, but honestly think that the two of you are good for each other. He wants to provide for you and give you the life we've always dreamed about."

"Yea, I know. I hope that I'm not out of my league though," she said.

"What do you mean?"

"I mean, I hope when I meet the other wives, they'll accept me into the fold and not judge me the way some of these trolls are doing," she responded.

"Forget about them! They don't know your life! People are always gonna believe their own narrative, but you and Javarius and those who love y'all know it's real. I wouldn't worry about those wives. I'm sure that you will fit right in that bougie little circle," I encouraged.

"I hope so."

"If you're uncomfortable, maybe me and Imani can go with you to your meetings until you're okay to go alone."

"I like that idea, but since I'm the only wife, I think I need to go alone until I find out what the rules are," Milani declined.

"Okay, well the offer still stands whenever..."

"I appreciate you sis," she said. "I'll let you know what the deal is when I find out."

"Okay. Well, I'll give you a call tomorrow. I think Jaylen is coming in the door," I said.

"Okay. Tell him I said hey."

"I will. Tell Javarius and Imani I said hello."

"I will. Love you sis."

"Love you more," I said.

We ended the call right as Jaylen was making his way in the door. I walked over and gave him a kiss.

"Hey babe, how was your day?"

"It was good. How was yours?"

"It was good. I just got off the phone with Milani. She said to tell you hey."

"Oh, okay. Tell her hello next time you speak with her," he said as we walked into the kitchen.

"Are you hungry?"

"Starving. I had four BBLs to do today. Did you cook?" Jaylen asked.

"Well, have a seat and I'll warm your food," I said as I took the plate that I had made and covered for him out of the fridge and into the microwave.

"So, anything interesting happen while I was at work today?"

"Interesting like what?"

I wasn't sure what he was asking me. I spent most of my day home looking up vacation spots and other things to talk to Jaylen about.

"Well, I saw a video online..."

I took the plate out of the microwave and grabbed him a fork out of the drawer. I poured him a glass of Scotch and placed the plate and drink on the counter.

"What video?" I asked.

"A video of your sister fighting some girl in the boutique," he said as he shoved a forkful of food in his mouth.

"Well, if you saw the video, then you know that she didn't start that fight. She was defending herself because the girl hit her first."

"You know babe, when you told me about you and your sisters' upbringing, I wanted to help you. I really wanted to save you because I thought that you were too beautiful to be living in some cheap housing project. That's why I offered to bring you and your sisters here to live," he explained.

"And I appreciate that. I've told you that several times."

"Yea, you did. Here's my point... you're married to a doctor now..."

"I know that."

"Do you? Because you are going to have to decide whether you want to carry yourself with class or if you want to remain hood," he said.

"Jaylen what the hell are you talking about?"

I had no idea where his mind was, but I knew he had me feeling some kind of way. I didn't want to think that he was trying to offend me, but it felt very offensive to me.

"You know when you hang with ratchet, ghetto people, it tends to rub off on you," he explained.

"Okay now, wait a minute! Are you calling me and my sister ratchet and ghetto?"

"Not at all..."

"Good!"

"But what I am saying is that when you hang with people who aren't in the same class as you,

you tend to get put in that category as well," he said.

"First of all, my sisters aren't ratchet, ghetto or whatever the hell else you seem to think they are," I said.

"I didn't mean to offend you..."

"Well, you did! I'll always be grateful to you for bringing me and my sisters here, but no matter what you did for us, that does not give you the right to speak to me the way you just did! My mom may not have raised us with a whole bunch of money, but she did shower us with love and taught us how to respect people and each other! Just because we don't act all bougie and stuck- up like the people you're used to being around, doesn't mean we don't have class!"

"I didn't say that babe," he said. "I just don't want people talking about you."

"I don't care what they say about me!" I snapped. "First of all, that chick put her hands on my sister first! What did you expect her to do? Not defend herself! Because I'm gonna be honest with you, if it had happened to me, I would have done the exact same thing!"

"See... that's what I'm afraid of. That you will be out there fighting and tussling with your sisters!"

"I don't need to fight for my sisters! When her and that girl got into the first fight at Javarius' house, I never jumped in and neither did Imani!"

"Wait, wait! First fight! You didn't tell me anything about that!"

"I did tell you!" I said.

I remembered having a conversation with him about all the drama that had happened that day. Now, he was telling me that I never told him about the fight. That was a damn lie!

"You told me about some chick that smashed Javarius' truck windows, but you never mentioned anything about anyone getting in any kind of physical altercation."

"Well, I thought I did tell you!"

"You did not! I surely would have remembered if you had mentioned that to me," he said.

"Well, it's in the past now. And even then, my sister was defending herself! Contrary to what you believe, me and my sisters do NOT fight with anyone unless they attack us first!"

"If you say so. At some point you are going to come to the realization that you aren't the same person from the hood that you were a month ago," Jaylen surmised with a serious expression on his face.

"Oh, don't get it twisted... I'm always gonna be that lil project chick from the hood. Just because you married me and upgraded my lifestyle doesn't mean that I'm no longer that person or that side of me evaporates. I'm still the same person that I was when you met me," I stated.

"Well, you're going to have to change that shit because it isn't working for us!"

"It isn't working for us or it's not working for you?" I inquired.

"I'm just asking. I've paved the way for you to have a better lifestyle than you did before. I just want you to take advantage of what this has to offer you," Jaylen said. "I just don't want people talking shit about my wife because I don't want to have to come out of character."

"Well, I think we both know that I don't give a damn what people have to say about me! I know who I am, and I'll always be true to myself."

"Okay, well, I'm gonna tell you like this... if you don't start to carry yourself in a classier way, I'm afraid our marriage is going to suffer," my husband informed me.

"What are you trying to say exactly?" I asked nervously. "Are you saying that if I don't change, you're gonna divorce me?"

I couldn't believe my husband was coming at me this way. "That's exactly what I'm saying," he confirmed as he nodded his head.

"Wow! Never in my life have I ever heard that a man divorced his wife because she is who she is. You knew who I was before we got married Jaylen!"

"And you knew who I was before we got married too Dior! I told you before we said 'I do' that I needed you to become more refined..."

"You mean boring!" I stated as I crossed my arms over my chest.

"Call it boring if you want to, but I'm a well-known plastic surgeon with celebrity clientele. How do you think that makes me look to have my wife associated with people who have a negative reputation and are constantly in the news?" Jaylen asked.

"Okay, now you're feeling yourself because none of this shit ever made it to the news! It was on a couple of blog sites..."

"That's negative shit and whether you want to admit it or not, a blog site like The Shade Room gets a hell of a lot of attention!"

"So, what you're saying is that if a bitch steps to me or my sister, we're supposed to back down so nothing negative doesn't make the news to tarnish your reputation! Keep in mind, her man has a multi- million- dollar career as well!"

"I don't give a shit what Javarius Johnson does for a living! What and who I care about are the two people in this house! So, in answer to your question, YES! If someone 'steps to you', I want you to back the hell down! I don't understand what part of that shit you don't understand?"

"I cannot believe you're threatening to divorce me!" I mumbled. "I haven't even done anything!"

"It's all about the company you keep babe."

"Well, you might as well divorce me then cuz I won't ever abandon my sisters! We came here together, and I made a promise to my mom ON HER DEATHBED that I would look out for them, and that's exactly what I plan to do! So, do whatever the fuck you wanna do, but if it comes down to choosing you over my sisters, it's never gonna happen!"

He sat at the counter chewing his food with a smirk on his face. I didn't know what the hell had gotten into Jaylen, but he had me fucked up if he thought he was ever going to come before my sisters. Promises may not mean much to some people, but they meant a lot to me.

How was I supposed to be able to look at myself in the mirror if I turned my back on Milani and Imani knowing the promise I made to our mom? I knew Jaylen had an important career, but he was acting as if I was out there shaking my ass in the club or fighting some random bitch who had stepped to me.

The only reason Milani had even fought that fucking girl was because she threw the first lick! I didn't know where Jaylen was from and I honestly didn't care, but if a bitch ran on me somewhere and slapped, hit, punch or even spat on me, I was taking her ass down and that was just what the hell it would be!

Yes, we were from the hood, but we didn't bring the hood out here to Vegas. However, it is still inside us and we will behave accordingly. I can sit up in these bougie ass doctors' wives faces and hold a very intelligent conversation with them that would have them drooling. But I could also handle my own with the messy heifers who wanted to get in my face.

"Be careful with your word choice," Jaylen warned.

"I see nothing wrong with what I said. Look Jaylen, I am not going to play these games with you. Is this why you wanted to marry me? So, you could turn around and divorce me a week later?" I inquired with a serious expression on my face.

"No, I married you because I want to build a life with you..."

"Yet after a week, you want a divorce! That makes no sense!"

"I can't have you running around with your sisters acting all hood and ghetto!"

"Oh no! You did not just call me hood and ghetto!" I had never felt so offended in my life.

I didn't even deserve to be called that shit! I hadn't done anything wrong, and neither had Milani.

"You need to take that back!" I blared.

"Dior just your name means that your mom wanted better for you. My guess is she gave you and your sisters those beautiful names because she wanted y'all to have nothing but the best in your future. I want that for you too, and I want your sisters to have it. I want to give you the life you deserve after having struggled for the past twenty-eight years. But if you want me to do that for you, I'm going to need you to make a choice," Jaylen said.

He placed the sheet of paper towel on the plate after wiping his hands and stood up. He walked over to me and kissed my forehead.

"Just think about what I said. Are you willing to give all this up for the life you left behind?" he asked as he looked into my eyes. "I'm going to go jump in the shower and get ready for bed. It's been a long day and I have an ever longer one scheduled for tomorrow."

Without another word, he turned on his heels and headed for the bedroom. I couldn't believe he was acting this way. What a fucking crock of shit!

He was so worried about himself and his reputation that he didn't seem to give two shits about what he was asking me to do! As I sat on the barstool, I looked at the video of my sister that had been posted online. It had over half a million views already and people were saying different things. Some were supporting her for fighting back, and others were saying some very negative and degrading things about Milani.

How can people make assumptions about my sister when they didn't even know her? She had every right to do what she did because had she not done it, that woman would keep coming for her. Some people were saying she should have been arrested too. I didn't think so and was glad that the cops hadn't arrested her.

I stood up and scraped Jaylen's plate before rinsing it and putting it in the dishwasher. Then I stepped outside on the balcony and dialed the number of someone whose voice I really needed to hear. With every ring of the phone, my level of anxiety grew.

"Hello," answered the voice on the other end of the line.

"Were you asleep?"

"Nah, just laying down. What's up?"

"I don't think I can do this," I admitted in a soft tone.

"Do what, babe?" asked Knox.

"This marriage! This whole fucking charade! I don't think I can do it!"

"Why? What happened?"

"He's a fucking jerk, that's what happened! Milani got in a fight today at a clothing boutique..."

"Yea, I saw that shit! She had every right to whip that bitch's ass!" Knox agreed.

This was what I needed. He always knew what to say and when to say it.

"Yea, that's the same thing I said!"

"So, what's the problem?" he asked.

"This muthafucka told me that I'm too ratchet and ghetto to be married to him!" I cried.

"The fuck! Yo, he really said that shit?"

"YES!" I fumed. "He said if I didn't leave my sisters alone, he was gonna divorce me."

"The fuck! Y'all just got married!"

"I KNOW!" I hissed through clenched teeth. "But fuck him! I'll tell you what I told him..."

"And what's that?"

"That if a divorce is what he wants, then he needed to go right ahead and file!"

"No, babe! That's not the plan..."

"Fuck the plan and fuck him! My sister married a baller, so I can move out and stay with her until you and I figure things out," I said.

"Ain't nothing to figure out Dior. I need you to stick to the plan and play nice," Knox encouraged.

"I don't wanna fucking play nice! This shit is too hard!" I complained. "It took everything I had in me not to cut that nigga in the throat earlier! I don't wanna do this anymore!"

"Babe, calm down!" he stressed in a soothing tone.

"I don't wanna calm down! I just wanna walk away from this whole situation!"

"Babe please, listen to me. Do you remember our conversation we had before you left?"

"Yes, but..."

"No buts."

"We had that conversation in bed after you dickmatized me! That doesn't count!" I argued, feeling my face redden.

"Sssshhhiid! Tell that to that purring kitty you got over there," he clowned, which caused me to laugh. "That's it, babe. I want you to keep feeling..."

I heard the glass door slide open, so I paused my conversation.

"Who are you talking to?" Jaylen asked from behind me.

"Imani," I lied.

"Uh huh," he responded. "Are you coming to bed?"

"Not yet. I'm still very upset about our earlier conversation," I replied honestly.

"Don't be upset babe. It's not that serious," he stated.

"It is that serious for me! You want me to choose..."

"Sssshhhh!" he shushed me like a child. "I won't have you speaking about our business like that, especially while you're standing on this balcony!"

"I don't understand what the big deal is. It's not like people are listening to us!"

"Do you know that for sure?" he questioned.

"No..."

"EXACTLY!" he stated. "If you want to continue this conversation, you're going to have to bring it inside."

I wasn't trying to continue this argument. This was just Jaylen's way of trying to control me yet again. Talking about people listening to us. Who the fuck was listening to us? I was sure nothing about this fucking conversation was worthy of someone eavesdropping!

"I don't wanna continue the conversation. You go on to bed, and have a good night," I said.

"Well, I would like you to come inside," he said.

"So, now you're trying to take away my freedom of choice?" I asked with an attitude as I finally turned to face him.

"What are you talking about Dior? Where is this hostility coming from?" he inquired. "I just asked you to come inside."

"And I told you that I don't wanna come inside right now!"

"You really are being difficult this evening. I wish I had seen this side of you before we went to the chapel!"

"And what's that supposed to mean?" I asked.

He didn't bother to respond to that question. He simply shut the door and walked away. "See the shit I have to deal with!" I said to Knox.

"Yea, and I'm sorry babe. I wanna just say fuck it, but..."

"I know. I hate this!" I cried.

"Hate what?"

"Everything! I hate being separated from you! I hate being apart from my sisters! I hate that our mom is gone! It just seems like everything is falling apart and there ain't a damn thing I can do about it!"

"It'll get easier baby. I promise."

"How do you know that though? You don't know that for sure!"

"I tell you what. How about I come to Vegas next week to spend some time with you?"

"What? Really!"

"Yea, really. Would you like that?"

"Hell yea! I would like that a lot!"

"Then it's settled. I'll come out there next week and we can spend some quality time together."

"Thank you so much!" I cried happily.

"You don't have to thank me babe. It's all love. Now go inside before ol' boy gets suspicious. I love you and we'll talk soon," Knox said.

"I love you too," I crooned into the phone as I batted my long eyelashes.

After I ended the call with Knox, I felt much better. I made my way inside and headed straight for the master bathroom. I turned the water on and when it was heated enough for me, I disrobed and stepped in. As the water cascaded over my head and down my tired shoulders, I tried to relax.

I turned on the shower radio and listened to the smooth sounds of Johnny Gill. That man knew he could sing! I lathered the loofa with some sweet, scented soap that Jaylen had gifted me before rubbing my body with it. I wished we could have gone on a honeymoon too, but Jaylen was too busy to take any time off... at least that was what he told me. I just knew a trip out of the country would have made me feel better about things.

That nigga had a lot of nerve calling me and my sisters' ghetto and ratchet. Like bitch if that was how you felt, you shouldn't have married me. I hated when rich men or women married people and thought they could just change and dictate their lives to suit them and their lifestyle. If he wanted a spoiled, bougie and stuck- up wife, then he should have married one.

I was more than sure there were plenty of women who fit that description in his life before I came along. Why the hell did he want to marry me so badly? Now that we were together and married, he was trying to mold me into someone I wasn't.

I knew how to act classy and bougie, but that wasn't me. I wasn't ghetto and hood either. I was just a big town girl who had it hard growing up. I promised myself that if I ever got out of the projects that I would make something of myself. I would do better.

I would never toss my sisters to the side for anyone, especially not a man! Sure, Jaylen was good- looking and he was fine, but he wasn't the best in the sex department. At least twice after we had sex and he had fallen asleep, I had to whip out my dildo and call Knox for him to help me get where Jaylen had failed to take me. It wasn't that he couldn't take me there. It was just that he got there first and forgot that I was on the road with him.

Shit, I wanted to get mine too!

As I stood in the shower listening to Johnny serenade me, I thought about Knox and the good sex we had before I moved to Vegas. He was such a skilled lover and the way he ate my yoni always made me scream for more. Just thinking about him had me touching myself.

I was on the verge of cumming when Jaylen walked in and asked, "What the hell are you doing Dior?! I could hear you all the way in the bedroom!"

"Just taking a shower!" I replied breathlessly.

"Well, can you keep it down please?!" he asked rudely. "Some of us have to work in the morning!"

Once again, I didn't bother to say anything to him. I couldn't believe he had interrupted me right before I...

"Oh, and by the way, I don't know what the hell you doing to yourself in here when the monster is in the bedroom," he flirted with a chuckle before he walked out and shut the door.

His words made me cringe. Little did he know that I didn't want him at all. This marriage was a fucking farce! I knew it and he knew it too! That was why it was so easy for him to ask me for a divorce.

After I finished my shower, I felt good. Not as good as I would have felt if I had been able to reach heaven, which was where I was trying to go before Jaylen rudely walked in. But I felt better than I did before I stepped in. I knew it was because of Knox. He always knew what to say to get me smiling.

I just needed to remember that I had a goal and in order to reach that goal, I needed to keep Jaylen happy.

Chapter twelve

Imani

Four days later...

Milani and Javarius had left for Jamaica yesterday, so I came over to stay with Dior while they were gone. I did not expect her and Jaylen to get into an argument about me being here, but I heard them in their bedroom. I would have liked to believe that I wasn't the reason for their argument, but I heard my name being said way too many times for it to not be about me.

When Dior reentered the living room, I said, "I didn't mean for you guys to start fussing about me being here. If you want me to leave, I can go back to Javarius and Milani's house. I just didn't want to be alone in that huge house!"

"You don't have to leave Imani. I'm sorry I made you feel as if you did," Jaylen said. "I was just caught a bit off guard because MY WIFE didn't mention to me that you would be staying with us for a few days. But you are more than welcome here!"

"Thank you," I said with a smile.

"You're welcome. Now, if you ladies will excuse me, I have a couple of things I need to take care of."

"You're leaving?" Dior asked.

"Yes."

"How long will you be gone?" she asked.

"I'm not sure."

"Okay. Be careful."

"Will do!"

Without another word, he grabbed his jacket and headed out the door. "Damn! Are you sure you want me to stay?" I asked.

"I'm positive, but I'm gonna need you to cover for me if Jaylen gets back before I return."

"What do you mean? You're leaving too?" I inquired as I watched her slip her feet into her Gucci sandals.

"Yea. I'm sorry sis, but Knox is in town."

"What? I thought you were done with him!"

"What made you think that?" Dior asked.

"Oh, I don't know. Maybe the wedding band on your left hand maybe," I replied sarcastically.

She threw her head back and laughed. "Girl, you're so silly!"

"What am I missing?" I asked.

"I will tell you all about it, but not right now. I haven't seen Knox since we left Houston, and I am so excited right now! I need to see him. I need to feel him inside..."

"Oh, whoa! Whoa! Whoa! TMI sis!"

"Sorry Imani. I was just saying," she said with a huge smile on her face. She walked over and gave me a hug and kiss on the cheek. "See you in a few hours."

"What the hell am I supposed to tell Jaylen if he gets back before you?" I questioned.

"I don't know. Tell him I went to Jupiter." She giggled which caused me to laugh as well.

My sister was playing a dangerous game. She was married to Jaylen and from what I could tell, he was all about appearances. I wondered how he would feel or what he would say if word got out that my sister was having an affair.

"Can you at least tell me where you're going in case you turn up missing?"

"Girl, stop! I am not gonna turn up missing, but I'll send you the address. Knox rented us an Airbnb so that's where I'm going. I won't be long..."

"Yea, right!" I expressed.

"I love you!" she called out as she headed for the door.

"Love you too!"

This is crazy!

I came over here so I wouldn't be by myself, only to be left by myself. I headed to the guest bedroom, stripped down to my bra and panty and climbed in bed. I wasn't worried about Jaylen seeing me like this because I wasn't going to exit the room.

Seeing as how I had very little clothes on, I was going to make it my business to stay in my room for the rest of the night. I got comfortable in this nice big ass bed and turned on the television. I channel surfed until I just put it on *Law & Order: SVU*. I didn't even remember closing my eyes, but I must have dozed off because the next thing I knew, Jaylen was gently nudging me awake.

"What are you doing in here?" I asked.

"Do you know where Dior is? I just came home, and she isn't anywhere in the apartment," he said with a worried expression.

"She said that she was going out with some friends..."

"What friends? I didn't know she had friends out here," he said as he stared at me sideways.

"I think they're friends from back home."

"What friends from back home, Imani? This doesn't make any sense! I was under the impression that the only two people she spent time with were you and Milani! Now you're telling me she went out with some friends from Houston! She's not even picking up her phone!" he stated in a worried tone. "Did she at least tell you where they were going? Why didn't you go with them? I mean, since they're from your hometown, I would assume that you know them as well."

I didn't know what to tell this man. I knew exactly where my sister was and who she was with, but I wasn't going to tell him that!

"I don't know where she is. She just said she would be back soon," I lied.

"Was she still mad about the argument we had earlier?" he asked.

"I don't know. She seemed fine when she left."

"What time was that?"

"Jaylen, I don't know. I'd really like to give you more information, but I don't have any to give you," I continued to lie.

When I caught him looking at me strangely, I realized that my chest area was exposed with just a bra. I quickly covered up with the sheet.

"You don't have to be embarrassed. I see women's breasts, ass and pussy all day long. It doesn't bother me."

"It's still inappropriate for you to be sitting in my bed when I'm barely clothed," I said.

"Imani, please don't take this the wrong way but have you ever thought about getting your body enhanced?"

"What?!" I asked feeling insulted.

"I'm sorry if I offended you because I certainly didn't mean to. I was just asking about you and your thoughts. It's something I ask all my patients when they come in to discuss a procedure," he explained.

"I'm not your patient and I didn't ask you..."

"I know, but I'm just asking if you've ever thought about enhancing your body. I mean, I can do that for you. I can make your boobs bigger, and I can even add some extra to your behind," he offered.

"You've been looking at my ass!" I asked.

I was starting to think that Jaylen might be a dirty old pervert! What the hell was he doing looking at my ass when he was married to my sister?

"You are really sensitive, aren't you? I am a plastic surgeon, Imani. Looking at women's asses and boobs are part of my profession. I can assure you that I am not trying to put any moves on you other than to help you land your own rich man."

"I don't know if you're making fun of me or what..."

"I promise you I'm not."

"So, are you calling me unattractive?" I asked, hoping that wasn't what he was saying.

"No, not at all. I think you're a beautiful young woman."

That made me blush. Jaylen was the first guy who told me I was beautiful. Jaylen was the first guy who ever paid me any real attention. My sisters were always the ones who caught men's eyes. I guess their big round melons and their plump asses did that. They got my mom's ass, so I guess I got my dad's.

It wasn't that my ass was flat as a pancake. It just wasn't as round as theirs. I never thought about getting plastic surgery because I couldn't afford it. Now, Jaylen was offering it to me...

"How much?" I asked.

"How much what?"

"How much for the surgery?"

"You really think I'd charge you for that? You're family... we're family. I'm just trying to help you look your best. If you'd like me to help you out with that, just get out of the bed and I can tell you what I can do for you," he offered.

"You mean right now?"

"Why not?" he asked with a smile.

"Because we're the only ones here," I said.

"Don't you trust me Imani? Do you think I'd do something to hurt you?" he asked.

Maybe enhancing my body wasn't such a bad idea. After all, Milani and Dior had been getting men's attention for years. Meanwhile, I was still a virgin for whatever reason. Maybe it wouldn't hurt anything for me to have this surgery. I slowly slid out of the bed.

"Please don't make fun of my body," I warned. "I'm self- conscious enough already."

"I'm a professional Imani. I would never make fun of you," he said. I stood before him, and he stared at me. "Can you take your bra off please?"

"What? NO!"

"How do you want me to examine your breasts if they're tucked away inside your bra?" he asked with a serious expression on his face.

"Fine." I reached behind me and unlatched my bra hook. Then I removed it and placed it on the bed.

As I covered my boobs with my hands, he gently placed them by my side. As he cupped my breasts in his hands, he said, "Okay, looks like you're working with a C cup. Is that right?"

"Yea."

"See, I do know what I'm doing," he said with a smile. That kind of put me at ease a little. "So, how big would you like to go?"

"I don't know."

"Do you like the size of Kim Kardashian's breasts, Latto, Megan Thee Stallion? Let me know."

"I guess Latto's is fine," I said shyly.

Okay cool. You mind turning around," he said.

"Why?"

"So, I can look at your butt!"

"You think I need to do something to my butt too?" I asked.

"I just think you could use a little bit of a rounder structure. Turn around and let me see," he said.

The panty I had on showed a little of my cheeks, so it kind of embarrassed me a bit. "I've seen it all before, Imani. If we're going to work together, you have to trust me," he encouraged.

I turned to face the opposite direction and felt his hands on my behind. Never had I ever had a man touch my body this way. First my boobs, now my ass. What next?

"Yea, I could give you a rounder butt, but considering you don't have much fat from here to put back there, it won't be huge like Latto's. However, I can give you a rounder, plumper shape that will add volume to your buttock area," he surmised.

"Really!" I asked.

"Yea. When would you like to do it?"

"What? My sisters will kill me!"

"Don't tell them," he said.

"How can I have surgery and not tell my sisters, Jaylen?" I asked as I reached for my bra and put it back on.

"You're grown Imani, which means you can do what you want. I have an apartment downtown near my office that you can stay in to recover. That way your sisters won't be able to try to talk you out of it before you do it."

"What's the downtime for a surgery like that?" I asked. "Because there's no way I can hide from my sisters that long."

"Well, first off, these are two separate surgeries..."

"Two!"

"Yes. The Brazilian Butt Lift is one and it'll require you to lay on your stomach for about six to eight weeks. Once you have healed from that, you can get the breast augmentation. That requires you to lie on your back for another six to eight weeks, but I promise you, it'll be worth it."

"But that means I won't see my sisters for four months! And who's supposed to take care of me during that time?" I asked.

I mean, it all sounded good, but maybe it wasn't the right thing for me to do right now. Maybe my body wasn't as bad as I thought it was.

"I see you're having second thoughts. Get dressed," Jaylen said.

"What? Why?"

"I wanna show you something," he said. "Meet me in my office when you're done."

"Okay."

I didn't know what he wanted to show me, but I got dressed and went to look for him in his office. When I walked in, he was sitting at his desk on his iMac computer.

"Here. Come sit," he encouraged as he patted the seat of the chair next to him. I slowly walked over and took a seat.

He was working on a 3D body image. "What is that?" I asked.

"It's a 3D model of what your body looks like now," he explained. He turned the model to the side and said, "This is what your body looks like sideways." Then he turned it to the back, and I was so embarrassed. I must have had the world's smallest ass.

"Ugh! Does my body really look like that?"

"Yes. However, if I enhance your breasts to a double D cup size..." I watched with wide eyes as he extended the breasts in size. The side model looked well developed, so he turned it around to the front.

"Wow!" I exclaimed with a smile.

"Now, let me do the rear," he said as he enhanced the butt area.

"Whew, chile! You mean to tell me you can get my booty like that!"

"Yes. If you had more fat, I could give you bigger, but you only have a little. So, I'm gonna use what you have which will give us this."

"I like it!"

"I like it too!" he stated. "So, do you need more time to think about it or have you made a decision?"

"I want the surgery!" I spoke loud and clear. I was the only one of my three sisters who didn't have a life. I needed a life.

"Okay, so are you going to let your sisters know, or do you want to stay in the apartment?" he asked.

"I think I want to stay in the apartment you offered and just surprise them."

"Cool. How soon would you like to start?"

"Today!" I busted out laughing.

"You ready ready, huh?" he questioned as he laughed too.

"Why put off tomorrow what you can do today?"

"True, true. Well, give me a week to get everything together. I'll have one of my nurses tend to you after the procedure and I'll be checking on you every day."

"Wow! You would do all that for me?" I asked.

"Yes. My job is to help people feel better about themselves. What I noticed about you since the first time we met is that you lack the self-confidence that your sisters have. If these procedures can give a boost to your self- esteem, I want to do that for you," Jaylen said.

"Thank you! Thank you so much!" I cried as I threw my arms around his neck. I didn't even realize I was crying until I felt the tears on my cheeks. To be honest, I didn't think having procedures like these would make me feel so happy.

"You're welcome," he said as he held me close.

After several minutes, I finally pulled out of his arms because being there was feeling really good, and I knew I wasn't supposed to feel that way.

"Well, I'm gonna go back to my room now. Just let me know when you're able to do the surgeries and I'll be ready."

"Which do you want done first?"

"Which do you suggest?" I inquired, wanting to make the best decision for me.

"I suggest the butt first."

"Then the booty it is!" I cheered.

"I'll have my secretary schedule it tomorrow and call you with the details and date," Jaylen said.

"Thanks again, Jaylen. I really appreciate it."

"That's what families are for."

I smiled and walked out of the office. I rushed to my bedroom and jumped straight in the shower. That touch from my sister's husband had done way more for me than it should have, and I knew it wasn't right. As I stepped into the shower and turned on the water, I didn't even flinch when the cold water hit my skin.

I was too fucking hot to care! As I allowed the water from the huge square shaped showerhead above me to rain down on me, I wondered what it would feel like to finally have sex. It was crazy that I was almost twenty- two years old and still hadn't experienced my first orgasm.

I wondered how it would feel to do that for the first time, but I wanted to do it with a real man, not a toy. I wanted to feel a warm body on top of me and hear the slapping of our flesh as we became sweaty. I just hoped that with this new body Jaylen was going to give me, I would finally get to love on a man.

Chapter thirteen

Whitney

Two weeks later...

The past month had been hectic as fuck! I had been in and out of court because of all this shit with Javarius and his new bitch he called wife. I didn't even know where that hoe came from, but I sure wished she would go back.

I had plans for me and this man. Then she came around and threw a whole monkey wrench in my fucking world. I hated her and wondered how Javarius could have fallen for her so quickly. Like the week before they got married, he was in bed with me and my friend!

I didn't like sharing Javarius, but he liked having threesomes. I wondered if he was having foursomes now since he had two of his wife's sisters living with them. I didn't know what the deal was with her, but I needed that bitch gone... and I had a plan.

It broke my heart to see him enjoying his time with her in Jamaica. I had never been to Jamaica before. That was a trip I would have liked to have been on, but instead of taking me, he took HER! Seeing pictures of them frolicking on the beach while holding hands and sipping on fruit drinks all day hurt my feelings. I hated to scroll on Instagram because it seemed as if everybody was talking about the "happy couple".

The Shade Room and these other blogs had beautiful pictures of them doing various activities and of course, it had me all in my feelings. But after wrestling to get out of bed for the past couple of days, I finally went to Walgreens and bought a pregnancy test. I knew I couldn't be pregnant because Javarius always insisted on using a condom when we had sex.

If I was pregnant, Lord please don't let me be. But then again, this could work out in my favor.

I got the test and headed home. I couldn't wait to get there to take it so I could find out if I was or wasn't. A pregnancy at this time would not be a good thing, but it could possibly help to slow things down with Javarius and his marital future.

I rushed inside the apartment and closed the door. I opened the package as I walked towards the bathroom. By the time I walked into it, I was holding the stick in my hand. I sat on the toilet and put the stick under the stream of pee I had flowing from my coochie. Once it was saturated, I placed it on a piece of toilet paper and rested it on the counter.

After I dried myself and flushed the toilet, I stood at the sink and washed my hands.

KNOCK! KNOCK! KNOCK!

I rolled my eyes and shut the bathroom door before going to see who it was. I pulled the door back and there stood Glen with his mouth full of good teeth and a huge smile.

"S'up baby!" he greeted as he kissed my cheek and walked in.

"What are you doing here Glen?" I asked.

"I just got back in town, and I wanted to come check you out. I haven't seen you in a couple of months. You good?"

"I'm great! How've you been?"

"I've been good. I been thinking about you though," he said as he reached for me.

"Oh yea? What you been thinking about?" I asked as I moved out of his reach.

"That good pussy girl!" he said as he bit down on his bottom lip while staring at me the way the big bad wolf looked at Lil Red Riding Hood.

"Well, I've been thinking about that dick too..."

"Yea, then let's make them two clash..." he said as he approached me.

"I would like to but I'm kinda in the middle of something. You think we could probably meet up later?"

"Yea, yea! You gon hit me up when you done with whatever you got going on?"

"Sure will."

"Gimme a kiss," Glen said as he grabbed me and pulled me close to him.

He pressed his lips to mine and stuffed his tongue inside my mouth. Lord! This boy was about to make me say fuck that pregnancy test and give him some pussy right now. What should have been a simple kiss until later turned out to be an extremely hot kiss that had my pussy biting my panty to get some action.

I finally was able to separate my lips from his and fanned myself. "Whew, boy!" I expressed as I leaned against his 6'1 slim frame.

"Lemme bust that thang thang open real quick!" he said. "I know you want it."

"I do, but I got some business I need to handle first. I promise when I'm done, I'll hit you up so we can finish what we started."

"You promise?"

"Yes, that's what I just said."

"Aight."

He pecked my lips again with his big juicy ones and walked out the door. I leaned against the door for a couple of minutes trying to catch my bearings and get my knees to stop quivering. Finally, I was able to calm myself down enough to walk back to bathroom. I looked at the stick on the counter and saw the 'plus' sign.

Now, I was both nervous and excited. Excited to be pregnant and nervous because I was going over to Javarius' house to inform him. I wasn't sure what he would say about that. I knew his bitch would be pissed, but it was what it was. I wasn't sure how far along I was, but I hoped it was far enough for him to believe the baby was his.

I grabbed the test and dropped it in a snack bag before jumping in my car and heading over to Javarius place. I couldn't wait to tell him the news, but when I got there, I was in for a shock. As I pulled up to the entrance and guard shack, I smiled at the dude named Perry because I just knew he was going to open the gate to let me through.

He came up to my driver's side window and smiled. "Hey Perry," I flirted.

"Hey there, Whitney."

I waited for him to lift the arm of that red and white stick that sat across the way because it was keeping me from getting where I needed to be. But he didn't. He just stood there and smiled.

"Uhm, what are you waiting for? Open the thingy," I said.

"Well, if you're going to visit Mr. Johnson, we've been ordered not to let you through. However, if you're going to visit someone else, I just need their name, address and phone number to confirm."

"What the hell you talking about Perry? You know the only person I know back here is Javarius! Now, please let me by or call him! Do what you gotta do but let me back there cuz I got some news for him!" I fussed.

"I'm sorry Whit! I can't do it. I hope you don't take this personal, but my job is at stake here!" he said as he smiled and shook his head from side to side.

"Perry please just let me through! I'm asking you nicely," I said.

"And I'm telling you that I can't do it."

"I thought we were friends."

"It ain't about us being friends. It's about me doing my job so I don't get fired! I got four kids, so I can't afford to lose this job!" Perry informed me. "Now, if you don't leave, I'll have to call the police, and I really don't wanna do that."

"Well, when you call them, you can tell them to meet me at Javarius Johnson's house!" I stated.

"I told you I'm not picking up the arm..."

"It's okay boo, I ain't ask you to!" I stated as I floored the pedal and busted through that white and red arm.

The shit broke just like when Madea drove through it on the movies, but I could tell it did some damage to my car. I really wasn't trying to get in trouble again, but I had to tell Javarius the news. I heard sirens somewhere, but I was determined to get to my destination. However, I didn't make it there because as I rounded the curb, I forgot to brake and lost control of my fucking car.

"GOTDAMMIT!!"

To be continued…

Made in the USA
Middletown, DE
05 July 2023

34598454R00116